The Lake House

OLIVIA MILES

R

ROSEWOOD PRESS

ISBN: 979-8986262499 (print)
The Lake House

This is a work of fiction. Names, characters, businesses, places, events and incidents are either the products of the author's imagination or used in a fictitious manner. Any resemblance to actual persons, living or dead, or actual events is purely coincidental.

ALSO BY OLIVIA MILES

Blue Harbor Series

A Place for Us

Second Chance Summer

Because of You

Small Town Christmas

Return to Me

Then Comes Love

Finding Christmas

A New Beginning

Summer of Us

A Chance on Me

Evening Island

Meet Me at Sunset

Summer's End

The Lake House

Oyster Bay Series

Feels Like Home

Along Came You

Maybe This Time

This Thing Called Love

Those Summer Nights

Christmas at the Cottage

Still the One

One Fine Day

Had to Be You

Misty Point Series

One Week to the Wedding

The Winter Wedding Plan

The Briar Creek Series

Mistletoe on Main Street

A Match Made on Main Street

Hope Springs on Main Street

Love Blooms on Main Street

Christmas Comes to Main Street

Harlequin Special Edition

'Twas the Week Before Christmas

Recipe for Romance

The Lake House

1
LISA

The call came shortly after nine o'clock on what had started as an otherwise typical Friday morning. The gift shop that Lisa had run for the past seven years was quiet, the glass-paned front door not yet unlocked, the smell of her morning coffee rising above the perfumes and lotions and candles in seasonal scents that she'd been unboxing and setting up on a table near the front window. By habit, she checked the phone screen before answering, pausing only long enough to determine if she had enough time to quickly run an internet search of the number in question before taking the call.

Now was not the time for a call with her mother, who, on any given day could be living anywhere from Vegas to Argentina. Her sister Rachel was a licensed therapist and more fitting for that role. Or Ashley, who had less on her plate and a more carefree attitude.

Lisa eyed the laptop on the shop counter eagerly, then, deciding that she did not have time to look up her mother's current whereabouts at about the same time she recognized the area code as one from Michigan, she frowned and answered tentatively.

"Mrs. Anderson?"

Technically, legally, Lisa was still Lisa Anderson-Smith, having never changed her name back after her divorce, but she decided to let this complication slip and said, "Ms. Anderson. Mrs. Anderson is my mother." Or she had been, a long time ago. Unlike her, Lisa's mother had reverted to her maiden name within a week of her divorce being official. She wanted to start over, she'd announced with emboldened defiance. To shed her old life. That included the name. The furniture. The house.

And the summer house in Michigan, which Lisa quickly gathered was likely the purpose of this call.

"This is Wendy Patterson, from the rental management company. There's no easy way to say this, but I'm afraid that something has happened to the property."

Lisa felt her pulse quicken. "Has it burned down?"

She didn't know why that was the first thing that popped into her mind, other than the fact that she'd stayed up later than she should have last night, watching one of those made-for-television suspense movies that kept her company on the lonely nights since the divorce when Maisie was sleeping over at her father's house. She could already picture the insurance check arriving in her mail. Could fantasize about the sum she would see in that little box on the right-hand side. Could nearly taste the relief that it could buy.

Her fantasy ended when the woman on the other end of the phone snorted in shock. "What? No. Thank goodness, nothing like that."

Nothing like that. There went that dream. But not the problem. Which meant that in addition to all her other troubles, Lisa now had a new one to deal with. Fabulous.

Carrying the now empty box to the far side of the room, Lisa sank onto her upholstered stool behind the walnut countertop that went along with the French country theme of the shop. She pushed aside a boxwood topiary and reached for a pen and notepad, wishing that she'd had the common sense to let the call slide to voicemail after all.

"I'm afraid that when we went in to get the house ready for the season, we saw that the last renters weren't as careful as we'd hoped, despite our usual background checks, and we had a particularly harsh winter that caused some damage to the roof. I'm afraid we'll have to let the renters that are lined up know about the change in the condition of the home, but I can't imagine that they'll want to continue with their plans, especially as there are other options available on the island."

Of course there were, because the island was remote—too remote for some—all the way at the northern tip of Michigan, surrounded by the cool, clear waters of Lake Huron. Once it had been Lisa's favorite place in the world. But that was a very long time ago.

Lisa twirled a ballpoint pen in her hands. A trick she'd been doing since she was a child and fancied becoming a majorette in a band one day. It was one of many life plans that hadn't worked out. "We could probably offer them a discount—"

"I'm not being clear. Some of the repairs are outside of our scope. We're a rental management company, Ms. Anderson. We take care of little things. Lightbulbs. Appliance maintenance. But your house—"

"It's not my house," Lisa corrected. "It's my parents' house." Technically, it was her mother's house, having been passed down through her family, but again, there was no reason to get into their personal history and all its drama, even though half the island probably heard the gossip sixteen years ago. It was her mother's house, but her sole responsibility. It had been agreed upon early into the dissolution of her parents' marriage, along with the fact that Lisa's father would be moving down to Texas, and Lisa's mother was welcome to the city apartment that had once been the family residence. The summers on Evening Island were halted, and Lisa's mother had no desire to return.

Being naïve, or maybe just plain old optimistic at the time, Lisa had offered to handle it. The responsibility up until now had been minimal: a few emails and calls with the caretaker over the years, the collection of deposits and rental income, and the outflow of checks for repairs and maintenance from a designated account.

She'd done it because she'd loved that house. Because she'd wanted to pass it down to her daughter someday.

But that had been idyllic. A fantasy, maybe. And reality was setting in.

"Well, you are my point of contact," Wendy continued. "I'm afraid we cannot continue to take on this property until it's been repaired to its previous condition. And I would strongly suggest that you—or your parents—tend to it at the earliest possibility. I can suggest some contractors for the water damage—"

"Water damage!" But wait. Lisa sat a little straighter. "Well, if it's as bad as you're claiming, then I suppose I should call the insurance company. Do you know any demolition crews?"

There was a long pause before the woman hooted in laughter. "Oh, I'm sorry to mislead you. No, nothing that catastrophic, I can assure you. But, with a leaking roof comes mold, and then of course there are the floorboards that have warped, and... Well, I do urge someone to return to the island and see for themselves."

Lisa hung up the phone and set her head in her hands. She had a business to run, a child to raise, and a stack of bills that were already keeping her up at night.

Returning to Evening Island had never been a point of discussion, much less a desire. And now, well, now it was simply impossible.

* * *

At five o'clock, Lisa admitted defeat for another day and turned the sign on the door, telling herself that the rain had kept people at home and that tomorrow would certainly be better. Maybe she'd sell the new hand-carved candlestick set she'd just unboxed that morning. Or maybe the garden tools imported from Belgium. With their copper handles and hefty price tag, they weren't exactly practical, but then nothing in her store was based on need. It was based on want. It was a little jewel box in the center of her small suburban town, an escape from the mundane, a sanctuary for the weary, who were looking for a little pick-me-up, a treasure to set on their mantle or bedside table, a special gift for a special person, or, often, an impulse purchase.

But one set of gardening tools, however pricey, wouldn't cover the store rent, and if sales didn't pick up soon, the lovely grey-blue front door would soon be locked for good. And then where would that leave her?

The worry was still on her mind when she pulled into her the driveway of her small but cozy Tudor-style home ten minutes later, happy to see her daughter's purple bike leaning against the outside of the detached garage, even though she knew that Maisie was counting down the months until she could get her driver's license. Too many nights Maisie was at her father's—a consequence of having never worked out a formal custody agreement, Lisa supposed, even if Maisie was happier being where she pleased on any given day and Steve's condo was only an eight-minute walk from the house they'd once shared.

She let herself in the back door, depositing her bag in the small mudroom just off the kitchen. Maisie sat at the round table, in the same chair where she'd once sat on her knees for a better vantage, the same chair where she'd stared with wary eyes while Lisa tried to convince her to eat her broccoli. Now, Maisie's long legs were crossed, her shoulders hunched, her nut-brown hair, which sometimes felt like the only thing she'd inherited from Lisa, a curtain hiding her face.

She didn't look up when Lisa stepped over to the sink and washed her hands, drying them on one of the imported hand towel sets that hadn't sold two seasons back. Lisa always tried to keep the inventory in her shop fresh, knowing it was the only way to ensure her regular clients returned week after week, especially since they were the only ones keeping the lights on in the shop.

"Don't tell me you're already starting your summer reading packet!" Lisa teased. "How was the last day of school?"

"Good... Hey, Mom," Maisie said distractedly, scribbling something into her notebook. "Is it okay if I spend the night at Dad's tonight?"

"Again?" Lisa tried not to show how disappointed she was when she opened the fridge and hid her face inside. She'd thought that maybe they'd get some ice cream to kick off the start of summer.

"For dinner then?" Maisie asked. "You could join us. Dad won't mind."

Far too many nights, Steve still joined them for dinner, years after he'd moved out of this house they'd bought when Maisie was about to start kindergarten—a last-ditch hope at the life they thought they wanted, a second chance for the family they'd never quite become.

It had been seven years since the divorce, and, as her youngest sister Ashley liked to point out, she still hadn't moved on.

And, as her mother liked to point out, she wasn't getting any younger.

Her middle sister, Rachel, the couples' counselor, had much more to say on the matter, but Lisa didn't need her advice. She knew that everyone was right, even though she was only thirty-five.

That was another thing her mother had been right about, back when Lisa announced that she was marrying Steve, when she was only twenty years old, still in college. Her mother had predicted an unhappy ending, and she hadn't been shy in saying so.

Now, Lisa looked at her daughter, who had Steve's bright blue eyes and wide smile, and decided that her mother was wrong. She had Maisie, and she couldn't have imagined any other outcome.

"I thought we could order a pizza tonight, maybe watch that fashion show you like so much?"

Maisie stood up, looking nervous. "I have to talk to Dad about something. But...I wanted to tell you first."

Lisa snapped the fridge door closed, her heart hammering in her chest. Oh, no. Not something big. Please no. She'd known that the day was coming when the real parenting issues would start, when she'd long for the days when her biggest concern was a lost show-and-tell toy or a squabble on the playground. She stared into her daughter's big eyes, hedging her bets. A bad report card? A date with an older guy? One with...a motorcycle?

For a moment, she almost wished Steve were here to handle it with her, but she quickly pushed that straight out of her mind. Steve was a good father and co-parent, but he was far from her emotional support person.

Or he should be, at least.

"You know how I've wanted to go to France since I was, like, five?"

Lisa breathed a little easier and smiled. "Of course. We both have. Don't worry, I'm still planning to take you for your sixteenth birthday." A nagging worry made her stomach tense up for a moment. That was still months away, yet getting closer. She'd tucked away a bit every month, ever since the divorce, but recently, she hadn't been able to scrimp as much as she'd hoped.

"I went ahead and applied to this summer program. You have to write an essay and show your transcript and, well, I got accepted! I'm going to France this summer!" Now Maisie was squealing and jumping up and down, and thrusting a piece of paper at her.

Lisa blinked at the signature line that Maisie was referencing, trying to cover her shock. And maybe, selfishly, her disappointment. For years, France had been their dream. Their trip, just the two of them. It solaced her in the lonely months—and even years—after Steve moved out. It gave them something to talk about, right down to the guidebooks that they'd often flip through, always thinking of another place to add to the itinerary.

And now Maisie was going to France. Without her.

"You're not mad, are you, Mom?" Maisie asked quietly.

Lisa rallied. She had no choice. "Of course I'm not mad. I'm proud! And excited for you!" She swallowed hard and willed herself firmly to not cry.

"And we can still go together for my birthday. Just as we'd planned!" Maisie grinned.

Lisa sighed, giving her a smile. She hoped she could keep the pain out of her voice. "Of course we will!" Even though it wouldn't be anything like they'd planned now. "Now, tell me where I have to sign."

"You have to sign right here. Or Dad. And I need a check. For that amount of money. From you. Or Dad." Maisie pointed to a sum that made Lisa's stomach roll over. Usually, she and Steve shared expenses when it came to these things, but in this case, she knew that Steve would cover it if she asked him to, maybe even if she didn't.

"Not a problem," she said lightly, but her jaw had become tense. Her daughter was going away for the summer. To France. Without her. And between the shop and the cost of this trip, she didn't know how she was going to cover it all.

Not to mention the other setback. The darn house on Evening Island. A house that belonged to a family that no longer existed. A house that was now her problem alone.

2
RACHEL

The argument today was about the dogs.

Rachel nodded her head, trying her best to keep her gaze from drifting to the clock that she kept discreetly wedged between two picture frames on the shelf behind the couch where her patients sat.

Often, she intervened, posed a question, and challenged the couple to communicate, to listen, to understand. But there were some people who just never should have gotten married. Her own parents were a prime example.

While the wife began tearfully accusing the husband of favoring one dog over the other, and the husband countered with a justified accusation that his wife loved the dogs more than him, Rachel discreetly flicked her eyes to the shelf and breathed a sigh of relief.

"I'm afraid our time is up for today. Until our next session, I suggest you do something constructive with the dogs, together. A long walk perhaps." Fresh air and a long hard run was her answer to most things in life.

Neither of her patients looked pleased with this remark as they moved from their opposite ends of the couch and stood, still bickering as they left the small office. Their voices trailed down the hall while Rachel held back, checking the fat planner that sat on her desk.

Marty wasn't due back from Seattle until late tonight, and aside from the charity event tomorrow, there was nothing else scheduled for the weekend. Usually, that made Rachel twitch. Relaxing wasn't exactly her thing. But now she saw it as a way to work on the self-help book she'd been writing in her limited spare time, especially with a fall deadline now rapidly approaching. With a smile, she picked up her pen and filled in all the white spaces on her planner with exactly that. Satisfied that her time would be spent usefully rather than wasted, she strained her ear for any more sounds of discourse from the hallway and then went around the small room, flicking off lamps and shutting down her laptop.

Downtown Chicago was busy at this hour, but rather than go home to an empty apartment, she decided to stop off at her favorite restaurant for a much-needed glass of wine and some carbs—a guilty pleasure she enjoyed on the Friday nights when Marty was usually getting in late from wherever work took him that week.

Lawrence was behind the bar when she arrived at the bistro a brisk walk later, still wearing her silk blouse and pencil skirt.

"Rachel." Lawrence grinned. "Marty out of town again?"

"As always." She smiled, proud of her husband's success in the tech world. "A glass of my usual, please."

"Of course."

She fished her phone from her black leather tote bag as he slid the glass to her, and sipped the drink while she skimmed her personal emails and texts. One from her sister Lisa, asking her to call, which wasn't very typical. Nothing from Marty, not that she expected as much. They rarely, if ever, communicated while he traveled, or even while he was in town. They both understood the importance of each other's careers. Conversation could be saved for the end of the day, or in this case, the week. That's what weekends were for.

Rachel looked out the window onto the sidewalk patio, which was filling up with couples young and old, laughing and talking and leaning into their tables under the leafy trees that lined this street.

A flicker of something she didn't really want to analyze made her frown, and Rachel decided that this was the best opportunity to call her sister. They rarely spoke, and saw each other even less, even though Lisa lived only twenty miles outside of the city.

Their lives couldn't be more different. Rachel was married. She and Marty had demanding schedules, professionally and socially, even if they were all tied together. And Lisa was in full parenting mode. Running a little shop since the divorce gave her something to do, but it hardly came with the same stress that Rachel endured day after day, and sometimes, Lisa couldn't understand that.

Still, her sister had reached out. And Rachel had a full evening spread before her. She'd call this fate if she believed in such a thing, which of course she didn't.

Removing her black blazer and adjusting the cream, chiffon blouse underneath, she pulled up her sister's contact on the screen and tapped it before she could change her mind. Lisa answered on the first ring, and before she had a chance to exchange pleasantries, Rachel said, "Instead of chatting over the phone, come meet me for dinner."

"In the city?" Lisa's response wasn't a surprise. Despite growing up not far from where Rachel now lived, Lisa had left the city as a teenager and never showed a desire to return. She had instead chosen a very safe and suburban lifestyle, her short train trips took place exactly twice a year: at Christmas for the German market and a musical, and in the summer, for Rachel's birthday brunch.

Could Rachel analyze this as a reaction to their halted childhood, to the fact that certain things brought back uncomfortable memories that were often easier ignored? Sure. But Lisa was a creature of comfort and routine, and Rachel understood that all too well.

"It's only twenty minutes on the train," Rachel pointed out, knowing that there were express options on weekdays. "And it's rush hour. They must be leaving every half hour. Unless you have Maisie," she said, not that she'd mind if her niece joined them.

"No, Maisie just left to go to Steve's," Lisa said. There was a long pause. "I guess...I could meet you."

Rachel was surprisingly pleased as she gave her sister the address and hung up. Only then did she remember the urgent tone of Lisa's text asking her to call. Other people's problems she could handle, including Lisa's. But she could only hope that this problem didn't include her, somehow.

* * *

Nearly an hour later, Lisa walked into the restaurant, looking a little lost as she stood near the doors, taking in the crowded space. Rachel lifted her arm and waved, trying to flag her over, noticing the long, flowery skirt that made her sister stick out even more than the wild look in her eyes.

The city intimidated Lisa, from the fashion to the crowds. Remembering this, Rachel leaned forward and placed the dinner order with Lawrence, knowing that her sister would be relieved not to have to study the menu.

"I ordered us a salad to share and two pasta dishes," she said when Lisa finally made it to the bar and climbed up onto the stool, adjusting her billowy skirt under her legs.

"Wine?" Rachel asked, lifting her glass.

Lisa shook her head. "I have to drive home from the train station tonight." She looked around the room. "This place is something."

It was cozy with warm wood tones and dramatic artwork in gilded frames. "It's one of my regular spots. My apartment building is just two blocks up." Rachel gave her a knowing look over her wineglass. "You'd know this if you came into the city more often."

"Says the woman who wouldn't deign herself with a trip to the suburbs."

"Hey, I came for Maisie's birthday," Rachel retorted.

"Two years ago," Lisa said with a thin smile. She sighed. "I guess one glass of wine will be okay."

"You rebel," Rachel chided, and they shared a smile. With the order placed, she leaned back against the velvet stool, knowing that Lisa had something on her mind. "So, what brings you all the way down here? And I know it's not to see me."

"You know it's not that," Lisa said, looking sorry. She smiled as Lawrence handed her the glass of wine before nodding at Rachel, confirming she'd want another. "But I'm a mother. It takes up all my time."

Rachel had heard this a lot over the years, and always felt a little judged by her decision not to have children, or maybe she was just being sensitive. Either way, she said now, "But Maisie is getting older. And she's with Steve half the time."

Lisa met her eyes. Of course. That was a topic that Rachel didn't want to get into. In her opinion, Lisa and Steve still spent entirely too much time together, even if it was under the guise of doing what was best for Maisie. Seven years later, and to the best of Rachel's knowledge, Lisa hadn't been on a single date, even though Rachel had suggested a few men to her.

"She's going to France," Lisa said, her voice cracking.

Not following, Rachel breathed a sigh of relief that Lisa's troubles had nothing to do with their younger sister or—worse—their parents. She smiled easily. "And you don't want her to go?"

"It's not that I don't want her to go. It's just... We had planned to go together." Lisa shook her head and brushed away a tear. "I sound really immature, I know. You don't have to say it."

Rachel set a hand on her sister's arm. The trip to France had been discussed for years, always causing Rachel to feel a little sad, thinking of the semester abroad that Lisa had given up to marry Steve and then start a family so young.

Seeing the sadness on Lisa's face now confirmed Rachel's own choices.

"You sound like a woman who loves her daughter. It's not easy letting go, and Maisie's getting to that age..." She'd worried about this for her sister. Yes, Lisa had the gift shop, but her entire world was Maisie. And what would happen when Maisie went to college, never to return, only to move on with a career of her own, or eventually settle into a marriage?

Marty and she talked about this frequently, always nodding their heads in firm agreement that they had made the right decision not to have children, not to build their lives around someone else, but instead, to find that same sense of fulfillment in something that didn't grow up and move on and away. Their careers weren't going anywhere, and their possibilities were infinite.

Their salad arrived and Rachel plated herself half. "How long will she be away?"

"A month," Lisa said miserably. "I mean, she's so excited, how could I say no?"

"You couldn't," Rachel agreed. "But Lisa, look at it this way, for..." She tried to remember Maisie's exact age and failed. Another reason she never truly considered the idea, she told herself. "You put Maisie first every day, and now you have four weeks to focus on yourself. Maybe go out on a date. Take a trip. When was the last time that you had a real vacation? And I don't mean Disney World."

"I like Disney World," Lisa insisted. "You would too if you gave it a chance."

"Me?" Rachel laughed. "Honey, you know Marty and I are—"

"A power couple, I know." Lisa pierced a lettuce leaf. "Besides, it wouldn't be any fun to take a trip without Maisie."

Warning bells went off in Rachel's mind but she resisted the urge to give any advice. Her sister wasn't looking for answers right now. She was looking for comfort. And Rachel knew that her role right now was as a sister and not as a therapist.

Really, it was a refreshing change.

"You could always take a trip with Mom," she chided, and they both laughed. Last they'd checked, their mother was living in the Bahamas, with her boyfriend of the month, sometimes of the year, if things went smoothly. Those relationships never panned out, but each time she met someone knew, she still dared to hope that it would last.

Rachel didn't know whether to be worried or envious of her mother's ability to still believe in love after what their father had done to her—staying back in the city to have an affair while they all summered at the lake house, blissfully unaware that by fall, their family would never be the same again.

"I'll figure something out," Lisa said. "I have no choice. It's just that...I'm not like you, Rachel. I wouldn't be comfortable having dinner by myself in a nice restaurant like this. You don't ever feel lonely?"

Rachel's heart sped up a little as her sister's gaze searched her face, and she flashed a grin, picking up her wineglass.

"Lonely? How could I? I'm surrounded by all these people—"

"They're strangers," Lisa replied.

"Not Lawrence." She shared a smile with the old man as he crossed behind the bar. "Besides, I'm with people all day long. By the end of the day, I'm happy for a little peace and quiet."

"But weekends," Lisa said.

Rachel took another slurp from her glass. "Endless schmoozing. Dinners. Charity events. You know how Marty's business is. It never ends. Besides, I have my book. My work never ends."

"Maybe you're the one who needs the vacation then," Lisa said with an easy grin, as two plates of pasta were set in front of them.

It had been a long time since she and Marty had been away, Rachel realized. She couldn't even calculate when it had been, and she made a note to check her personal planner when she got home tonight.

Home to her empty apartment. Which was all the more reason not to go home at all just yet.

She glanced at her sister and smiled. "I think we deserve some dessert tonight. Chocolate. What do you say?"

"I guess I have nothing to get back to," Lisa replied slowly.

And neither, Rachel thought with a pang, did she.

* * *

Rachel hailed a cab for Lisa and gave the driver clear instructions before checking that Lisa had enough cash on her for the fare.

"You're forgetting that I'm older than you," Lisa said ruefully, but Rachel could sense her gratitude as she opened the car door.

"Hey," Rachel said through the open window. "You didn't ever tell me why you texted."

"Oh." Lisa frowned for a moment and then brushed her hand through the air. "It's nothing, really. Just a hard day. I wanted to connect."

"Well, I hope I succeeded in making you feel a little better."

"You did. And that chocolate cake for dessert did too."

Rachel was still smiling as the cab pulled away, and she began walking toward her apartment building with a strange sense of optimism. She didn't see her sisters enough, and unlike Ashley, who lived in New York, there was no excuse for Lisa. She'd have to make a better habit of it. She'd add it to her planner, tonight.

She checked her watch—a Christmas present from Marty three years ago—and calculated that he wouldn't be landing for another hour, meaning she had time for a soak in the tub and maybe a few chapters of her new thriller.

The city was busy at this time of night, the lights glowed from within the restaurants and bars that lined both sides of the street. At the next crosswalk, she paused for the light and soaked in her surroundings, reminding herself again that all this buzz and chatter and stimulation was exactly what she wanted, and couldn't give up.

The restaurant closest to her now had changed hands recently, and, deciding that she probably had another thirty seconds before the light changed, she moved closer to the window to have a look. Her eyes snagged something as she approached. Her cheeks flushed with heat as her heart began to speed up, leaving her a little breathless.

There, at the bar, was a hand with a watch, exactly like the one she'd given Marty, three years ago last Christmas. And it was resting on the shoulder of a very thin, very blond woman in a very red dress.

She told herself she was being silly. Irrational. It had been the wine she'd had over dinner. At her usual place. The place that Marty knew she went to every single Friday. Alone. Because she knew Lawrence. Because she didn't really want to be alone at all.

Because Marty was out of town. En route.

Except that he wasn't. The man had curly brown hair and a fine-cut suit, and when he turned, as if feeling her stare, and glanced ever so briefly over his shoulder before returning his attention to the woman at his side, she let out a little yelp.

Rachel pulled back from the window, caught the walk sign that was now flashing from across the street, and dashed toward the other side, toward her towering brick apartment building, the one that she'd carefully chosen over all the others in the city, the one that was supposed to be as indestructible as her marriage, which only now felt just as lonely.

3
ASHLEY

Ashley Anderson was what one might call a "professional bridesmaid," and this weekend her services were once again required. Standing in an itchy gown in a color that was a strange cross between coral and peach that she most definitely wouldn't be wearing again—unlike last weekend's wedding, where the bride had put everyone in navy, knee-length dresses that would become a staple in her closet for future rehearsal dinners—she clutched the bouquet of mixed flowers and smiled as the photographer clicked his camera for the hundredth time in ten minutes, checking his shots before nodding and finally allowing the group to disperse.

Ashley's gaze roved the grounds of the park where tonight's festivities were being held, estimating that it was about a hundred-yard walk to the tent and the flutes of crisp champagne that were being passed around on silver trays. Her poor feet had suffered this long; she could make it.

The bride—one of her many friends from college who had

ended up engaged to her frat-boy boyfriend about a year after graduating—stood back with her now groom, looking radiant in her white chiffon gown as her veil caught the evening breeze and floated behind her just as the photographer lifted his camera.

"She makes a beautiful bride," Ashley said wistfully as another friend from college, and a fellow bridesmaid, waddled up beside her. Eight months pregnant, Trina's special day had been last April, a lovely affair in Manhattan, at one of the best hotels in Midtown, too. Gold bridesmaid dresses. Possibly, something that Ashley could wear again. Maybe for New Year's Eve or a holiday party.

Trina gave her the same look that she often received. "And so will you. By my calculations, you're next in line."

Ashley frowned. What Trina had said was true. Their friend group from college was all paired off now. The days of vacationing together, even for bachelorette parties, were officially over. Unless Ashley gave them a reason for one more hurrah.

"We'll have to plan another girls' trip soon," she said, shifting topics off her nonexistent love life.

Now Trina looked at her with a snort and pointed two fingers to her large bump. "I think those days are behind me. This was my babymoon, and my ankles are so swollen that all I want to do is go back to the hotel room, take a cool bath, and order room service."

They'd reached the tent by now, and Ashley plucked a glass of champagne from the nearest waiter while Trina dropped into the closest chair, one that wasn't assigned to her. The dinner would start soon enough, and then they'd be expected to sit at the head table, all the girls lined up, all reunited yet again.

But for the last time?

The champagne didn't roll down her throat as nicely as it should, and there was a sour taste in Ashley's mouth. These women were more than her friends. They were her family. They'd stayed up late on countless nights, talking, laughing, sometimes crying, sharing all their hopes and dreams and secrets and fears. Ashley knew that Trina had wanted to marry Tony DiCampo from the moment she first saw him across the quad during freshman orientation. And now she was about to start a family with him.

Ashley's heart began to race as the magnitude of that settled. All this time, these girls had been her family—her replacement family, when her own had broken up, or shattered, really. But now they were starting families of their own. And she was left standing alone. At a wedding with no one to dance with, in a dress that didn't exactly complement her particular shade of blond. In pointy, too-tight shoes that probably wouldn't allow for much dancing anyway.

She moved across the reception tent, admiring the details that had been put in place. She knew all the trends. One would think that she'd be bored of weddings by now, but she still enjoyed them. Made her living off them too. The wedding blog that she'd started after college, when she'd first been graced with the title of maid of honor by her friend Leila, who had married Chase from across the freshman dorm hall, had taken off over the years. Now, she had advertisers and sponsors, and she'd even been featured in a prominent magazine last fall.

She was a wedding expert, falling back on beautiful, inspiring photography, with tips and trends and lists. She knew what was in, what was out, and what was absolutely overdone. Even if she'd never had one of her own and never planned to, either. Because even though she'd never say it, not even to these wonderful women who had stood by her for all these years, she didn't really buy the product she was selling. Sure, right now Trina was happy, with a baby on the way, and she had married her college crush turned sweetheart. But so had Ashley's sister Lisa, and look at her now. Divorced. A single parent. For all Ashley knew, she hadn't even been out on a date in five years but instead spent the nights that Maisie was with her father sitting home alone, or working in her shop.

And look at her parents. The catalog-worthy family, the kind of stock-photo image that she often used for her blog. A handsome, affluent couple with their three daughters, who wintered every year in Vail and summered every year in Michigan. They'd had the storybook life from the outside until Ashley's mother had sniffed out the infidelity and the cracks began to grow from the inside.

Now Ashley's father was on his third wife. Her mother was on her hundredth boyfriend. And they hadn't spent another Christmas in Vail or summer on Evening Island since the Big Split, as she liked to call it.

So while Ashley loved a good wedding, she saw it for what it was: a party. And a wedding and a marriage were two very different things.

"Ah, another chocolate fountain," a deep voice said, coming up behind her.

Ashley grinned and took another sip of her champagne. Michael Green was one of the groom's friends. An outlier in her college social circle, but a regular face all the same, and not just because they'd been doing the same wedding circuit for the last few years. Michael Green was also a familiar face on the mornings after the weddings, and from the gleam in his bright blue eyes, this weekend was turning out to be no different.

She didn't mind. Looked forward to it, actually. They both knew the deal. They saw each other every month or six months or even once a year, depending on how the invitations fell. If they were both single—which they usually were—then they kept each other company while all the other couples paired off onto the dance floor. They were having fun. Making the most of a weekend away. It was an arrangement and one that worked out nicely, for both of them.

"I like the chocolate fountains," she said now, even though she did think they had probably run their course and she knew that her readers did too. What would be the next big thing? Classic fondue set up at every table? Cupcakes had come and gone, but they could always make a comeback. That's how life worked. What went away always found a way to come back again. Like Michael. Handsome, clean-cut, no-strings Michael.

Her fake date. Her nondate. Her good-time guy.

"I think they make the nights a little more...interesting." After all, it often gave her something to do rather than sit at her table and watch everyone else dance the night away. Find a strawberry and submerge it in chocolate. A slice of pound cake, ditto. It was amazing how many things tasted better smothered in chocolate.

He raised an eyebrow in that way that she had always found so appealing and said, "And here I thought I was the one making these wedding reception nights a little more interesting."

"Oh, you give yourself too much credit," she teased and started to walk across the uneven lawn toward the head table, where she would be seated on one side, near the bride, and he would be on the other, near the groom.

The head table: proof that some things never went out of style. And that some trends lasted longer than a marriage ever could.

"Are you we going to have a nightcap tonight?" he whispered from behind her, his breath so close that it tickled her ear.

She was stopped near a group of chatting people who showed no signs of going to their seats. Looking at him with a smile, she said, "I assume you're here alone?"

"Not much changes in a month," he said, referring to their one, excellent night last weekend that had ended with breakfast in bed and a checkout time that was dangerously close to the eleven o'clock cutoff.

Reminding herself of this, she stiffened a little. She'd slipped last time, let things go on a little too long. Chatted too much, laughed even more, and...enjoyed herself more than she'd told herself she could.

"A lot can change in a month. Or a week. Overnight even." She stopped herself. She was getting too serious for this type of setting. Too serious for this audience. Michael wasn't the kind of person she could open her heart to—no man was. She had her girls for that. The women who were now paired off with their husbands.

Their preferred confidants, she realized, glancing back at Trina, who was laughing with Tony.

She swallowed back another sip of champagne. "I have an early flight."

A shadow of something passed through Michael's gaze. Something that gave her pause. Something that told her that she really should stop side-stepping this conversation and just tell him flat-out that tonight wouldn't work. That tonight her door was closed.

But then she glanced over at the bride, coming down the lawn on the arm of her groom, and over at Stacy, who had been married since the fall. (Crimson bridesmaid dresses—one of Ashley's favorites.) A familiar feeling, and one that she had managed to keep at bay most days now reared, and there was no more champagne being passed around as everyone was starting to sit down for dinner, toasts, and speeches.

It would be a long night. A lonely one. Or...it could be a little less lonely.

She looked over at Michael as the group blocking their path to the head table finally dispersed.

"Meet me near the chocolate fountain after they cut the cake?"

He gave her a lopsided grin. One that made her question her sanity for even considering rebuffing him a few moments ago.

"Last wedding's cake was only a seven. If this is an eight or higher, we're staying for seconds."

"I can't argue with that," she remarked. But then, wasn't that the nice part of their arrangement? They got to have all of the good parts with none of the bad. No fights, squabbles, or disagreements.

No, this was better. They both knew where they stood. They had a good time, and when the wedding weekend was over, they went their separate ways.

He shoved his hands into the pockets of his tux and moved toward the right of the room, while she took the path to the left, biting back her smile.

* * *

The cake was only a six. Disappointing, but Ashley wasn't in the mood to prolong the evening anyway. It had been a long day, in very uncomfortable shoes, and she'd spent the last half of the toasts imagining how wonderful it would be to ease them off her heels and wiggle her toes.

Michael was waiting for her at the chocolate fountain when she all but hobbled up to him.

"I'm ready to call it a night," she sighed. "Of all the weddings I've been in, these win the prize for worst shoes."

"And here I was hoping that you might want to dance."

It took a moment for Ashley to register that Michael was actually serious. She noted the disappointment in his eyes that seemed to mix with some strange hope and immediately took a step backward.

"In these heels, no way." She managed to laugh, hoping to lighten the mood, but Michael inched toward her, his voice low.

"So, take them off. No one will mind."

"I will. I'd mind." Ashley wasn't talking about the thought of dancing barefoot at a wedding. It had been done before, of course. She was talking about dancing in general. With Michael. Michael who was suddenly asking for more than she could give.

"Being barefoot? Or dancing?" He looked injured. "I see. You don't want to dance with me, is that it?"

"Of course that's not it," Ashley said tersely. But it was. She knew it, and now he did too. "Isn't it more fun to sit and watch everyone else dance?" They'd had their share of laughs when some of the guests were especially uncoordinated.

"So that's what you want to do. Sit and watch everyone else dance, kiss, get married?"

Oh boy. Ashley felt her stomach swoop with panic. "Let's not ruin things. We have a nice thing going."

"I thought so." His jaw pulsed as he jammed his hands into his pockets. "I guess I thought that we might take it a little further."

"You know I'm not looking for that." She stared at him, hating that it had come to this, that he had to go and make things complicated.

"I guess I thought...I thought that maybe you'd change your mind."

This was why she didn't get close. Why she thought that Michael was a safe choice, a fun time, someone who understood.

Because when emotions got involved, people got hurt.

"It's not you," she said, but Michael shook his head.

"You say that, but it's not true. Someday someone's

going to come along and make you believe in something real. I'm just sorry that it wasn't me."

Ashley winced as she watched him walk away. "Michael!"

But he just kept walking, shook his head, and held up a hand, a gesture of goodbye. An end to a conversation. To the evening. To whatever it was they'd had. But not what they might have had.

Michael was a good guy. Handsome, fun. But she didn't feel anything more than disappointment that they'd argued as he disappeared out of the tent.

Ashley picked up a shortbread cookie and ran it through the chocolate fountain while the band picked up and the crowd cheered at the next song. She ate it slowly, savoring the sweetness, while she watched couples laugh and sway to the beat. The bride and groom were in the center, gazing into each other's eyes in a way that made Ashley almost believe that their love could last.

Almost.

Michael wasn't ever going to make her believe in the notion of a happily-ever-after, but no one else would either.

4
LISA

The Saturday night crowd at the neighborhood restaurant was a stark contrast to the seen-and-be-seen establishment that she'd been at the night before. Lisa should have been settled and relaxed at their usual table on the outdoor patio. Instead, her sister's words kept rushing back, making her feel uneasy as she studied the menu.

"You can't possibly be needing to look at the menu for this long." Across the table, Steve's grin was good-natured, but Lisa felt her back go up.

"Just wondering if there's anything I've...overlooked," she replied as she set the menu down again. It was Steve's night with Maisie because they did try to alternate Saturdays, but like all holidays and special events and even not-so special events since the divorce, they were spending it together. As a family. For Maisie. That's what they'd always said and that's what she'd always told herself.

But did she believe it?

Lisa reached for her glass of wine as the waiter approached.

"Ladies first," Steve said gallantly, as he always did.

Maisie ordered one of the daily specials and Lisa, as she knew she would, ordered her usual.

Across the table, Steve grinned. Because he knew she would too. And that was just the problem.

Steve knew her. Not just what she liked, but what she did. What she would do. He knew her well enough to know that she would come tonight because it was on the family calendar, the one that had been set up to organize their split time with Maisie, which had only resulted in more time spent together rather than apart. Maisie was their only child. She would be, Lisa knew, her only child ever. She wouldn't want to deny her daughter a special moment with her father any more than she would want Steve to exclude her. And so they celebrated the end of the school year. As a family. At least to outsiders.

"Just think. This time next week, I'll be packing for my trip!"

Lisa met Steve's eyes. She could see that he held the same trepidation, the same nerves about sending their fifteen-year-old across the ocean for a month. Same parental worries about where she would be, and if she'd be safe. She took comfort in that as she smiled at her daughter. The excitement in Maisie's eyes was contagious, and Lisa felt a moment of guilt for ever wishing her daughter had never heard of this trip, much less been accepted to the program.

"We'll have to have a send-off dinner!" Maisie said.

Friday was Lisa's monthly book club, and Saturday, while

technically her night, would again be shared. Not that she minded. Steve knew her longest. And unlike her sisters, he knew her best.

"Put it on the calendar!" Steve grinned as he pushed back his chair and straightened his long, lanky frame which hadn't changed much since college. "Let me wash my hands before I attack that breadbasket."

"Hey, it's mine!" Maisie laughed as she tugged the bowl of focaccia closer.

Enjoying the sounds of the familiar banter, Lisa pulled her phone from her bag, wanting to add the dinner to their plans before she forgot and no more reservations were available. Her heart skipped a beat when she saw the two missed calls from the property management company on Evening Island. Really, was there any more to say? She knew the place needed work. She appreciated the information. She also doubted that there was anything she could do at this point in the season to get things repaired in time to secure a renter for any weeks of the summer—maybe late August, at best, but only if she was proactive. And right now, she had other things to worry about. And other things to plan.

She'd need to take Maisie shopping, buy a bigger suitcase, make sure that she had international service on her cell phone, and all the other little things that she would need to live comfortably in a foreign country.

And the dinner. Of course, this warranted a good-bye dinner. Even if it was just for a month.

A month, she reminded herself, pulling up the calendar she shared with Steve. If Maisie was leaving on Sunday, then they might want to do a Friday dinner instead of Saturday.

She could give up her book club for one night, even if her neighbor, who was hosting, had asked more than once if Lisa would bring her famous cheesecake. She would still make one and drop it off, she decided—but her plans stopped there.

There, on Friday, below the little note listing book club in the pink color designated for "Mom" items was another item, in blue. A detailed item. One with a time stamp, and one that she hadn't added.

With a shaking hand, she tapped on the entry. A seven o'clock dinner at Bistro des Amis. One of the most romantic restaurants in the northern suburbs. One that she'd always longed to go to ever since it opened three years ago. Even Rachel had been, and Rachel never came to the suburbs, aside from Maisie's birthday, and not even every year.

Her heart was racing as the implication of what this meant unfolded, and she quickly turned off the phone and stuffed it back into her handbag at her feet when she saw Steve approaching.

Steve who had slipped and added a personal entry to their shared calendar. Steve who had a date next Friday. Steve who may have been dating for some time for all she knew.

Steve who was only going along with these family dinners for the sake of Maisie.

Steve, who, unlike her, had moved on.

* * *

Sunday was a busier day than most at the shop, especially at this time of the year, but despite the women who pushed through the door with smiles, browsed with murmurs of approval, and then thanked her for the time, the day didn't result in any sales. Not even of the brass gardening set.

At five o'clock, Lisa turned the sign on the door, but she wasn't ready to go home just yet. Maisie was at Steve's. There was nothing waiting for her at the house other than a pint of chocolate ice cream and a pile of laundry that she really didn't want to fold.

Besides, she had a stack of bills to go through, inventory sheets to review, and orders to place—or not.

It was the start of summer. Normally, with each change of season she refreshed her stock, but this year she saw little sense in that. And no means to pay for it, either.

She could have a sidewalk sale, she supposed. Next weekend. Get rid of all the winter items that hadn't sold, like the lovely cashmere robes that she herself would have loved to have received as a gift, but maybe not for that hefty price tag.

Trying not to panic, Lisa walked to the back room, which doubled as a storage space and her personal office, and sank into the oversized, upholstered swivel chair behind her large white desk. She could still remember when she'd set up this space. Her divorce was fresh, her future felt unclear and even a little frightening. The little storefront on Main Street with the sign in the window had felt like hope in a world that otherwise felt uncertain. She imagined filling it with beautiful things. Things you couldn't find anywhere else. Things that made you smile. Made you feel special. Maybe, even loved.

Now, even these four walls couldn't give her a sense of comfort. They only added to the feeling of loss.

Steve was going on a date. To Bistro des Amis!

She pinched her lips and tapped on her keyboard. She would not think about it. Not tonight. Not even Friday night.

Definitely not Friday night.

She skimmed her emails, trying to distract herself, her gaze landing on the one from the property management company with a heavy thud. It was a follow-up to their call on Friday, a list of repairs that would need to be made for the company to continue listing the house. With photos.

Lisa clicked on the attachments, her heart stopping at the first one. Water damage—extensive. Enough for her to know that this would be a pricey repair. It wouldn't come out of her pocket. It was technically her parents' place, but as the oldest child, somehow the responsibility and communication had fallen on her. Because she'd volunteered, years back. Because no one else had.

Maybe that's why she alone had cared. Until...she didn't.

The house was hundreds of miles away. A financial burden. A memory of a past life she'd rather forget and certainly couldn't dwell on now, not with all her parental responsibilities...

Except, for the next month, she didn't have any, did she?

Lisa tapped her nails on the desk and then, on impulse, dialed Rachel. She was almost surprised that her sister answered on the third ring.

"Hey, so I was thinking about what you said the other night at dinner."

"About dating?" Rachel was out of breath. No doubt on a run along the lakefront or on a treadmill at her swanky gym. That phone never left her side in case a patient needed her.

But right now, it was Lisa who needed her. Even if she couldn't quite admit that.

"About doing something with my time, when Maisie isn't around." She pulled in a breath. "I'm thinking of going to the lake house."

There was a beat of silence, long enough for Lisa to wonder if their connection had been dropped. "You mean Evening Island?"

Her sister's surprise gave Lisa the confirmation she needed. "It needs some work, apparently, and I'm hardly in a position to oversee it from here. I was thinking if we fixed it up, we might get a good price for it. The summer would be the best time to list."

"*Sell* the house?" Rachel was panting now, but Lisa could picture her standing still, with her hands on her hips, staring into the distance as she often did when she was thinking hard. Not much had changed in Rachel over the years—at least, not since the Big Split.

"No one ever goes, and I really don't have the time on my plate to worry about it."

"I guess I never thought about selling it. I guess I always thought..." Rachel didn't finish that sentence, but Lisa could finish it for her.

For years after her parents' divorce, Lisa had dreamed of them all returning. Of another summer at the big, old house facing the lake. Of nights that didn't grow dark until well after nine, spent sitting on the big porch, playing cards by candlelight, drinking lemonade and iced tea, munching on wild berries. She could still remember the sweetness in the air. The sound of the horses' hooves waking her each morning, and the soft breeze floating through her open window each night.

She'd always thought if they could just return, they could be a family again.

But they never had. And now it was time to accept that.

Time, she realized, to accept a lot of things.

"What about the shop?" Rachel, ever practical, asked.

"The shop can survive for a few weeks without me," Lisa replied. Really, what did it matter if she opened it or not? She wasn't making a sale, and the rent was due either way. She may as well use this time to cross one problem off her list. And selling that house would go a long way in giving her a nest egg she so greatly needed.

"What about Mom? Have you talked to her?"

Lisa snorted. "Have you?"

"Good point."

"Besides, Mom all but handed me the keys to that place. She hasn't bothered with it in years. She doesn't want it. I told her I'd keep it for Maisie but..." But Maisie was making her own plans now, and she'd continue to do that. Ones that didn't involve Lisa or the dreams she necessarily had for her.

"When do you plan to go?"

"Next Sunday," Lisa replied, impulsively. She'd leave right after she dropped Maisie off at the airport. "I don't think anyone will push back on the idea. I don't think anyone plans to ever return."

She could feel the weight of sadness across the silence, and this time she knew that she hadn't lost the connection.

"It's time to put the past in the past. Where it belongs," Lisa said, knowing that she was talking about more than the house.

"I'll join you," Rachel blurted, so abruptly that Lisa startled, wondering if she'd misheard. "Next Sunday. We'll drive up together."

"But—" Lisa fumbled. Rachel was the furthest thing from an impulsive person. Even further than herself. Yet here they both were, about to make the final trek to their childhood summer home. To say goodbye to it for good.

"Thank you," she said softly.

But as she hung up the phone and sat back in her chair, with the stacks of bills gathering dust on the desk and the photo of the water damage lit up on the screen in front of her, she couldn't help but wonder if, like her, Rachel had other reasons for making the long trip up to Evening Island.

5
RACHEL

The ferry from Blue Harbor departed at regular intervals for Evening Island during the busy season, and despite it being a Sunday, a day when Rachel had mistakenly assumed that most people would be returning to the mainland, the next two boats were booked solid.

"I knew we should have called ahead." Rachel cursed under her breath to the amused glance from Lisa. With a flash of irritation, she insisted, "We could be waiting another forty minutes. Maybe longer, considering it's peak season."

"You need to relax. We're on vacation. Not everything has to be planned in advance."

"Maybe not, but planning is one way to avoid confusion and chaos." And the one thing she'd relied on to keep her life running smoothly. The reassurance of looking at her planner, spread out before her, the events and appointments marked off with colored ink or sometimes, though she was almost embarrassed to admit it, stickers, never grew tired. If it was in her planner, then it was going to happen. It was something she could count on.

Except now when she thought about the art museum's gala next month, or the charity function for the children's hospital that she and Marty attended every August. She'd even scheduled her hair and nail appointments months out because then she wouldn't have to worry about looking the part.

Instead, she could worry about the fact that Marty might be taking another woman as his date. That instead of having to worry about people inquiring about their contribution, they'd have to explain their divorce.

Catching herself, she squared her shoulders. "I like knowing what I'm doing next week and next month. And definitely for today."

Lisa's eyebrows quirked. "Spoken like someone who never had a kid. You learn to wing it and think on your feet. And as for plans." She only laughed.

Rachel pushed back her temper, telling herself that Lisa wasn't trying to hurt her, even though she had. For years, Rachel had wrestled with the weight of her choices, which seemed to grow heavier with the passing of time. Whenever the thought took hold, she told herself that it was for the best—that children added stress and uncertainty—look at Lisa, for example. Instead, Rachel honored her agreement with Marty—so practical, so uncomplicated, so primed for success. She'd prioritized her marriage. And her career. Now, she wondered if she could salvage either of them.

Grateful for the sun that would last for many more

hours, Rachel hid her pain behind her oversized sunglasses and shrugged off Lisa's comment.

For someone who was equally guilty of not taking much downtime for herself, Lisa looked strangely relaxed, despite the seven-hour car ride with only one short pit stop. Her cheeks were flushed, her tortoise sunglasses cat-eye shaped and chic with that French flair that she'd always adored, and her linen joggers and tank top were wrinkled but enviably so.

By contrast, Rachel was still wearing her jogging clothes from this morning's run. She hadn't showered before the trip, because she'd gone three extra miles instead, hoping to outrun the noise in her head. Marty had been gone for the week—a blessing—but his return led to another Saturday spent just like the last: social obligations where Rachel had to keep up pretenses.

What would her patients think of her? What would her editor do? She couldn't exactly get a divorce before the book was released...or maybe not even immediately after. And did she even want a divorce? She'd been with Marty for ten years.

She should have known better.

In need of a distraction, she looked around, spotting a few shops and restaurants not too far from the dock. "I guess we could leave our luggage in the trunk and walk over to that café. Get something iced."

"Sounds nice," Lisa said, already leading the way.

When they used to come up every summer, they'd park their family car in this very lot. Sometimes they'd grab an ice cream while they waited for the ferry, or just find a spot in the shade, happy to breathe in the clean, lake breeze and stretch their legs.

Now, as Rachel joined her sister in walking toward the shops that hugged the water's edge, she saw that as much as everything looked exactly as she remembered it, a lot had changed, too.

"Firefly Café," she mused, looking at the building up ahead that shared an inviting porch with a bakery. She remembered the building, but the name had changed, and the store beside it was certainly different. "Buttercream Bakery. Now that sounds like exactly what I need."

"I thought you only ate sugar when you're stressed," Lisa teased before looking at her sharply. "Are you...stressed?"

"Me? Stressed?" Rachel laughed, because of course she was. When was she not stressed? Her job was demanding, her patients both a joy and a pain in the rear at times, and then there were all the events and dinners, mostly after work, or on weekends when she sometimes craved a chance to curl up on the couch in her favorite sweats, not that she could admit that to Marty. No, she and Marty had a deal, a pact as sacred as their wedding vows, even if they had been spoken in the courthouse instead of at St. Mary's up the road.

But now, Rachel wondered if that promise had been broken. She could have asked, confronted him, but hearing the truth would lead to action. And she wasn't ready. Not yet.

Besides, all too soon, Marty had taken off on another business trip, and then there was the dinner with the Jacobsons on Friday night, which always lasted too long, but Rachel had been grateful this time because it gave her an excuse to drop right into bed afterward, even if she didn't sleep that night. And then yesterday had been strangely routine. She'd gone on a long run, come home for a breakfast which was always spent in silence, each reading the newspaper over their toast and coffee, or sometimes something for work. Then Marty went to the gym and she went shopping for her trip and then they had that charity dinner at the Westin and well, she didn't really have to think of an excuse not to confront him. There was no time, not unless she wanted to make a scene in front of Jacobsons, who would have told have the entire Gold Coast neighborhood by this morning.

"Like you said," Rachel shrugged. "We're on vacation. And that drive was worse than I remembered." And sugar, though she didn't indulge often, was her comfort. Along with planning, but she'd already established that had failed her. Big time.

"That's because you worked the entire time," Lisa said as they walked up the path toward the bakery.

"It was better than listening to that book on tape. You and your French!" Rachel shook her head, even though she was always amused by Lisa's interest in all things Francophile. It certainly made for easy gift-giving, unlike her sister Ashley, whose passion was for weddings, even though she was yet to have one for herself.

Realizing that she hadn't even considered calling Ashley all week, she cringed a little. "Does Ashley know we're here?"

Lisa shrugged absentmindedly as she peeked through the window. "I left her a voicemail a few days ago. You know how she is." They exchanged a knowing glance as they entered the bakery. Their younger sister had always found more comfort in her friends over them, and since college, she rarely visited Chicago even for holidays.

"I doubt she'd care about the house anyway. She spent the least time in it of all of us, you figure," Lisa said, suddenly frowning, despite the unmistakable smells of vanilla and caramel and what could only be shortbread, freshly baked.

Doing what she did best, Rachel linked her sister's arm and jutted her chin at the overstuffed display case that was topped with cake stands and baskets, overflowing with scones and cookies and muffins.

"Do you think we should get a box to bring with us? The house won't have any food," she pointed out. And a remote island without cars didn't exactly lend itself to delivery pizza.

"Dessert for dinner?" When Lisa smiled it was radiant. "We're breaking a lot of rules on this trip."

Yes, Rachel thought, as she studied the bakery case with the longing of a child. But unlike her husband, she wasn't breaking the big ones.

* * *

They made it back to the parking lot just as the ferry was coming into port. Lisa popped the trunk on her key fob and reached for Rachel's top bag first.

"My goodness!" she exclaimed, grunting in the effort. "What do you have in here, a pile of bricks?"

"Books. For research," Rachel explained.

"You're planning to work while you're here?" There was a definite hint of disappointment in Lisa's tone that Rachel was too tired to analyze right now. If her sister thought this vacation was going to be a repeat of their childhood summers, riding bikes through town, wading through the cold, clear water, or building stone statues along the shore, she was mistaken. Rachel was on a deadline, and with a week away from her patients, there was no sense in letting such valuable time be wasted.

"I have to turn in this draft by September." Her heart began to race just saying the words aloud. "Besides, you'll be working too," she pointed out, giving Lisa an arch look.

"Oh. That's right." Lisa's shoulders sagged. "I got so swept up in the drive I guess I forgot about the house for a while there. And Maisie," Lisa said, chewing her lip.

"Nothing like a long car ride to make you stop worrying about her flight." Rachel closed the trunk and began walking to the dock. They could not miss this ferry, much as she wouldn't mind going back to that cute little bakery for a bit. She needed a hot shower more, even if it would be in a claw-foot tub. She needed to unpack, get her bearings, and do her nightly routine, even if it would be daylight for several more hours.

That was what had her so disoriented, she supposed. The time difference, even if it was only one hour. The sense of being so far north, the Great Lakes stretched out before them in a way that was so different than the feeling she had of Lake Michigan's city coastline. The air was so clean here that it filled her lungs, making her want to take gulp after gulp like she did with water after a long run.

She couldn't get enough of it, she realized. Even if soon she'd never have it back again.

They settled onto the ferry, selecting seats on the top deck so they had a full view of their surroundings. The sky was clear, bright blue, without a single cloud, and up ahead was the island, a big green mass high up above the water, the big white hotel visible as they approached, and then the other lakefront homes, some higher on the bluffs, others right down at the shorelines, a mix of colors, their gables poking through the dense trees, their architecture a nod to another time. A better time.

A time in her life that she'd banished. Looking backward led to sadness. Looking forward led to fear. But it also led to ambition. A desire to make everything up ahead better than what came before it.

She glanced at Lisa, who watched the island as it drew closer, wondering if she was thinking the same thing. If she, too, both longed for the past and feared for the future. If her life felt as uncertain as Rachel's did.

And if she remembered the last time they'd taken this boat ride together. Taking it for granted. She'd only been seventeen, not knowing then what would follow. That it would be the last time.

The ferry pulled to a slow stop at the docks where open windows from the waterside bars showed lively, happy people. A vacation mindset. If Rachel could just find a way to relax.

"Does it feel weird to you too?" Lisa suddenly asked.

"You mean almost like it was just yesterday that we were here?" Rachel nodded.

"I was thinking that it feels weird that it's just the two of us, instead of..." Lisa's eyes bore the regret that Rachel didn't want to feel.

Instead, she stood. Focused on the call of the gulls, the

wind on her face, and the rocking of the boat floor under her shoes. She moved forward and stopped just as suddenly.

A woman with shiny, blond hair that bounced against her back was holding an oversize tote—the same canvas style with the rope handles that their mother used each summer. For a moment, Rachel felt as if she'd seen a ghost. A vision of her mother in her younger, happier days.

"Wait," she said, grabbing Lisa's hand, not quite sure what she was looking at, even though it was perfectly clear.

Ashley was walking down the plank, dragging a pink suitcase behind her.

She and Lisa exchanged wide-eyed stares at the same time. So much for thinking this was going to be a chance to clear her head for a week. It was officially a family reunion. At the lake house, of all places.

6
ASHLEY

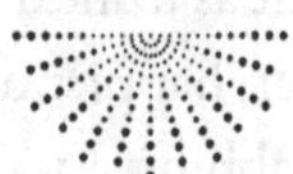

Ashley couldn't remember the last time she'd seen both of her sisters together. Wait. It was probably when Maisie was born, and that would have been...a very long time ago, she realized with shame.

She'd seen her niece since then, of course, when Lisa and Steve traveled to New York, but that had been before the divorce, which was practically ancient history, and since then... Well, since then Ashley had been busy. They all had.

Even if she'd been busy avoiding her family.

Standing on the dock, she embraced both of her sisters, sensing their confusion in the way their hugs were swift and stilted rather than warm and tight. But then, this was why she'd stayed away, wasn't it? Once there had been laughter and chatter and annual trips to this very island. There had been campfires with songs and ghost stories, fireflies lighting up jars, cool, crisp sheets and soft pillows, and the promise of another wonderful day in the sun. And then everything had changed, and gone were the good times. And the warmth. And the laughter. And even the hugs.

"Don't look so happy to see me!" Ashley stepped back and pushed her hair off her neck, wishing she'd remembered to wear a band around her wrist, but wishing more that she didn't feel that old pain in her chest, the one that was always there when she spoke to one of her sisters or her parents on the phone. Each time she connected with one of them, she dared to think that this time it could be different, better, and each time she was reminded of exactly how it was. But now, how it used to be.

"We're just surprised is all!" Rachel lifted her sunglasses to give her a proper smile.

"Well, I assumed I was invited," Ashley said with a shrug. "Lisa's voicemail said so, didn't it?"

Now she saw a look pass between her two older sisters, one that said that maybe Lisa had forgotten to mention that part. In other words, Lisa's invitation was empty. And no one expected Ashley to accept it.

And if Lisa hadn't caught her on a particularly bad day, when the rain was falling hard on the pavement and her cramped city apartment felt even smaller than ever, and she longed to get out, hang with the girls, only to make a few calls and find them all too busy with their spouses, then maybe she wouldn't have. Instead, she'd seen it as a sign, an opportunity presenting itself, telling her that there was somewhere else she was supposed to be right now. That she was right to keep Michael at arm's length—or any man for that matter.

At the time, she'd felt that Lisa had saved her from

herself. From more heartache. That somehow, from hundreds of miles away, Lisa had known her little sister needed her, even though it had been years since Ashley had ever asked for anything.

"Well, if both of you were coming back here after all this time, I wasn't about to let you do it alone. Or miss out." She didn't bother to mention that the entire plane ride here she'd wondered if she was making an enormous mistake—not in seeing her sisters, but in seeing this house. This island. Just stepping onto the ferry had sent a bolt of excitement through her that just as quickly turned to dread.

Now, her stomach fluttered with nerves. Would it all be the same? Would it be better? Would it be worse? She'd spent so long banishing the memories of this place that now that they started to come back, she was almost afraid to tarnish them. To see that the house wasn't quite as large as she remembered, or that the lake wasn't so clear and big. That all those shining moments of childhood were just an illusion, after all.

Just like they'd become that year they'd stopped coming, when what she'd thought was her perfect little family became nothing but shards, leaving her to wonder if they'd ever been happy at all.

"Well, of course, you couldn't miss it. The three of us. Like old times." Lisa looked so pleased that it took a moment for Ashley to realize that she hadn't seen Lisa without her daughter since Maisie was born. She devoted herself to her role as a mother, and completely changed her life, surprising everyone, Ashley knew. Especially their mother.

"Maisie's not with you?" Ashley looked over at the boat,

which was starting to pull back off the dock again, taking a bunch of weary-looking tourists back to the mainland.

"She's at a summer abroad program. In fact, she should have just arrived," Lisa said. She lifted her phone a little higher. "I still have a few bars and I doubt there's any service up at the house."

"Go on, check. Just because I know we won't hear the end of it tonight if you don't," Rachel said with a teasing smile.

Ashley watched Lisa walk away, feeling a little anxious at being left alone with Rachel, even for just a few minutes. Lisa was the mother hen, always had been, which was probably why she was so doting on her own daughter. Sometimes, when Maisie was little, and Ashley was just in her teens, she secretly wished that Lisa would adopt her, that she would raise her as her own. It was silly, really, and obviously impossible. But it had been a fleeting fantasy in those final years when she alone was stuck with her mother, being bounced around from city to city, or to her father's house and back again, the fallout of their marriage on naked display and her with a front seat ticket.

She saw and heard things that her sisters had escaped by luck of birth order and freedom that came with their extra years. And she didn't forget any of it.

"So," she said, dropping onto her suitcase, using it as a makeshift chair. She shielded her eyes from the sun with her hand, looking up at her middle sister, who hadn't changed one bit since she'd last seen her, when Rachel had been in town for a conference two summers ago. "I get the impression that you didn't really want me to come."

"Don't put words in my mouth," Rachel replied. "It's like Lisa said, we're just surprised. It's not like you've ever shown much interest in spending time together before this."

"I live in New York," Ashley reminded her.

"And it's much easier to get to Chicago from Manhattan than it is to get to Evening Island." Rachel's look was steady in that clinical way that made Ashley want to curl up or dash off, she wasn't sure which.

"No one has mentioned this island in years." The truth was that no one dared to, probably. "And the more I thought about it, it sounded like fun. Besides, it's true that the three of us don't spend much time together."

"And now's the time?"

"Now or never," Ashley said, then frowned. She supposed that's why she'd come, really. Not to spend the time with her sisters, but because there was an urgency to the visit. The last chance. And she needed it, even though she'd never considered it before. Maybe because she'd always thought that it would still be there. She checked her emotions for a moment before continuing. "So, you think the house will sell quickly?"

Rachel sighed deeply and cast her gaze out onto the water. "I don't know. Houses like that are expensive, and I can't imagine there are many buyers. But it's not like we have reason to hold on to it any longer."

No, Ashley supposed that they didn't, because she'd learned long ago that holding on to the past—to the memories, the places, and especially the people—just made it that much more difficult to move forward.

* * *

Lisa spent the entire carriage ride to the house talking about Maisie's flight, from what movies were shown, to what food was served, to the weather in Paris when she finally touched down, exhausted but elated.

Ashley listened with interest at first, and then out of politeness, and then she leaned back and took in the scenery. The main street, filled with shops and restaurants, and bars that hugged the port, gave way to a sweeping view of the dark blue water to their left, with colorful homes shaded by trees to their right. When she was little, this ride was her favorite part of the trip—even better than the bicycle races with the Morgans and the Taylors, the other little girls who summered on West End Road. This carriage ride was the start of something magical. Gone were the cars and the noise of the city. Here life was sweeter, simpler, and better.

She breathed in the clear evening air, feeling more optimistic than she had all week. Or maybe, all month.

"We'll have to play cards while we're here. On the front porch." She kept her gaze straight ahead now, as they came up on the big hotel, famed for being featured in a classic movie. Its swimming pool was one of her favorite places on the entire island—maybe in the entire world—and she could still remember begging her mother to buy her a day pass, or later, flirting with some of the seasonal staff until they opened the gate for her with a wry grin.

"Do you think any of the Morgans will be here? Or the Taylors?" Her heart leaped at the thought of reconnecting with the girls she'd spent so many days of her youth with, laughing and playing from sunup until sundown. "We should go over and knock on their doors."

"Well, Gemma will be here, I know that much for sure," Lisa said. "She moved up here two years ago, started dating Leo Helms, who took over some caretaking from his grandfather when Edward retired."

"It will be so good to see her again," Ashley said, even though it was also a little nerve-racking. Would any of the other girls be here? The summer people that had become like a second family? "I wonder if Ellie's here too. Or the Taylors." She realized how disappointed she'd be if she realized that, like them, the other families on West End Road had all but abandoned their homes.

Or if she'd be more disappointed to know that they'd had endless joy-filled summers together, without them.

"First, we're going to need to figure out dinner." Rachel lifted a white pastry box. "We bought a few things back in Blue Harbor, but they're probably better for breakfast."

"Don't worry about that." Ashley reached behind her and patted the canvas tote bag that sat on the back of the coach. "I have three bottles of wine, dried pasta, a few boxes of cereal, and some jarred sauce in there."

"And no milk?" Lisa laughed but looked at her in awe. "Look at you. More prepared than your older sisters. And you took a plane. We have no excuse other than poor planning."

Rachel seemed to bristle at that statement.

"I'm nearly thirty," Ashley reminded them. And not married, came the nagging reminder.

She pushed it aside as the driver led the horses around the

last bend and there, before them, was West End Road. The lake was to their left, a row of large, Victorian homes to the right, and up near the next turn, into the woods, was their cottage.

They all fell silent, only the sound of the horses' hooves clapping along the dirt road could be heard over the pounding of Ashley's heart, and for just a moment, she allowed herself to fall back in time and remember how this felt. To shed the everyday troubles behind. To forget about modern technology, cars, and all the other things that seemed to weigh down the weeks as they passed into months. To feel like she could breathe and run and have nothing or no one hold her back. To arrive at the lake house at long last.

And for the last time.

7
LISA

They stood at the base of the porch steps, taking in the great, large house that stood before them. A strange sensation passed over Lisa when she considered that this house had been not quite abandoned, not exactly forgotten. But it hadn't been a part of their lives or occupied much of her thoughts aside from the annual selection of renters, and now a part of her felt a sense of shame, thinking that it belonged to her—to all of them—and that it had been here all this time, waiting.

She glanced at her sisters, but they seemed equally lost in thought. Their own feelings were no doubt as mixed and muddled as her own, and now wasn't the time to be dwelling on old hurts or regrets. She'd learned a long time ago that there was no point in wishing for what might have been. Things happened that were outside of anyone's control. You just had to make do and carry on. It was this attitude that had gotten her through her parents' divorce, and later, her own.

With that, she hoisted her luggage by the handles and climbed the steps, her sisters following at a slower pace.

The key was in her tote bag, and she fished it out, sliding it into the aged bronze lock, surprised in a way that it still turned for her, and so easily. She noted the wicker furniture that backed up against the front living room window as she glanced over her shoulders at her sisters, who stood on the porch shoulder to shoulder, their honey-blond hair making it undeniable that they were related, even if they couldn't have been more different.

"Ready?"

She didn't wait for an answer as she pushed open the door, realizing only once she was inside that she had been holding her breath. She alone had seen the photos of the wear and tear, the evidence of years of semi-neglect, of a house once loved now forgotten. She was prepared for the worst, but what she saw was...home. The happiest home that she'd ever known, at least.

"It looks exactly the same," Rachel spoke first, carefully setting her luggage at the base of the stairs.

"Aside from the scuff marks on the walls!" Ashley cried out, pointing a sharp finger in accusation where sure enough, the pale-yellow walls leading up the staircase were nicked and marked, probably by renters hurriedly pulling their heavy luggage around the corner.

"And the floors." Rachel's mouth pinched with disapproval at the place beneath her feet, where the walnut stain had been worn away, covered in pockmarks from heeled shoes and lines from suitcase wheels.

"Nothing a rug can't cover!" Lisa wished she'd thought

to bring some stuff from the store with her, especially since it probably wouldn't ever sell. But she hadn't been thinking clearly, or rather, she'd been thinking about too much. About Maisie and her trip and Steve and... Well, her mind certainly hadn't been on this trip. And until this moment, the house had been the least of her worries.

"Who's going to fix all this?" Ashley said, pointing up to the spot on the ceiling above the stair landing, where the water damage that Lisa had seen in the photo now appeared in real life. It was darker and larger than she'd even feared, and when she stared at it long enough, it seemed to grow before her very eyes.

"Edward retired a few years ago and his grandson Leo was doing work on the place for a while," Lisa explained. She wandered a few feet down the hall, peeking her head into the living room with the big picture window and the furniture that was huddled around the large fireplace where framed photos of the girls at various ages were still on full display. "But he's an attorney by profession and he's getting his own riding stables business off the ground too, so, that's why I had to come back. To find someone."

"I'm sure Edward can recommend someone," Rachel said with authority that Lisa needed to hear. "Or Leo."

"That's right. Leo lives at Sunset Cottage with Gemma now," Lisa explained. The Morgans had named their house for the spectacular views that could be seen each evening.

She felt better knowing that someone she trusted was right next door, even if she and Gemma Morgan hadn't seen or spoken to each other since their last summer here, way back when they were just teenagers. Years ago, she'd heard through Edward that Gemma's sister Hope had settled in the Chicago area, along with the Taylors, from the robin's egg blue Victorian at the other end of West End Road. Now, she felt sad that they'd lost touch.

"We'll have to stop by first thing tomorrow," Rachel said. She grunted as she lifted her suitcase. "But first, I need a long, hot shower. I forgot how dusty these roads can be!"

Lisa had forgotten a lot of things—or rather, tried to forget, she realized, looking around.

"You don't want to walk through the house first?" Lisa skirted her eyes to the dining room they never used other than for the occasional game of hide and seek, where the heavy and dark antique furniture was all still intact, exactly as they'd left it the last time they'd locked up the house for the summer and took the ferry back to the mainland. It sent a chill down her spine at how much hadn't changed in all these years, even though so much had.

"There's time for that," Rachel said, but Lisa had the sense that Rachel, much like herself, was putting off the inevitable flush of memories that would come at every turn.

Already she could remember sitting on the window seat in that front bay window on rainy days, doing a puzzle with Ashley or one of the girls from the street, casting an eye to the sky, just searching for the sun to appear through the clouds. It always did, even if she had to wait for it.

With a heavy heart, she picked up her own suitcase. "A long, hot bath does sound good."

"It does," Ashley chimed in as they all trudged up the stairs. "So don't go using up all the hot water."

"I'd nearly forgotten about that," Lisa said with a laugh

that lodged in her throat. It hadn't been a problem when they were younger, but as they grew older their mother was constantly pleading with them to save some of the water for the rest of the family.

She supposed that she hadn't had to think about her family's needs in a long time. Half a lifetime, really. When the family fractured, it was like everyone just fended for themselves, desperately grabbing for life vests in the only way they knew how.

Rachel dedicated herself to her school and, later, work. Ashley emersed herself with her friends. And Lisa had Steve. And then Maisie.

She sighed deeply as they made their way to the top floor, where now the spot on the ceiling was even more obvious. Below it, the wood was warped and discolored.

The doors were all closed, the only light pouring in from the oversized windows on the stair landing, and all of them seemed to pause, none of them quite ready to turn a knob and enter the bedrooms of their childhood summers.

Lisa looked to Rachel, who stared straight ahead at her door with laser focus and knew then and there that it fell on her as the oldest to lead the way. She'd brought them all here. She would have to see it through. And maybe, even find a way to enjoy it one last time.

"First one in the bedroom gets the shower first," she said with a flash of a grin as she sprinted to the closest door to the right, Ashley nipping at her heels.

The doors all opened and closed in a flurry, and muffled laughter could be heard through the walls. And just for a moment, as Lisa leaned her head back against the paned wooden door and closed her eyes, it sounded like the old days. The good ones.

* * *

Ashley, who had nabbed the first shower, was already in the kitchen when Lisa emerged half an hour later, feeling refreshed and even optimistic as the smells of warm tomato sauce brought the house back to life. The windows in most of the rooms she passed by were cracked open, allowing the lake breeze to float through, and it wouldn't be long before the sky turned all shades of pink and peach as the sun set over the water.

"The kitchen isn't damaged, at least," Lisa observed from the doorway. The room was always sun-filled, large, though a bit dated, which was even more obvious now. The cabinets were still in good condition, considering the numerous renters who had passed through. The table near the back door still housed six Windsor chairs, painted white. The butcher block where they always kept a bowl of fruit was bare. It was strange, being back here after so long. Details she hadn't thought about now seemed familiar, as if they'd been tucked there all along, like a lost book whose story you'd read a dozen times.

She crossed the room now and looked out the window over the sink, onto the backyard and the carriage house at the back of the property. Her phone pinged, pulling her from the scene with a jolt.

"You have coverage here?" Ashley looked almost alarmed. One of the perks of coming to this island every summer was the escape from the modern technology that consumed so much of their regular lives.

Lisa was as confounded as her sister. "Maybe Gemma managed to arrange some sort of connection when she moved back?" She pulled out her phone, seeing only one, fading bar. "Or maybe not. Maybe this section of the house is the only spot with service."

"Maisie?" Ashley pulled one of the pots from a lower cabinet and began filling it with water. Because Rachel was still in the shower, it came out slowly, but Ashley just used the time to stare at her expectantly.

Lisa had managed to connect with Maisie at the docks. This text, and the three before it that she'd seen down at the pier, were all from Steve.

"Just Steve."

Ashley arched an eyebrow. "Steve as in your ex-husband Steve?"

"And the father of my only child, Steve." Lisa crammed the phone back into her pocket, even though she doubted she'd be hearing from Maisie again soon, and not just because of the limited cell service. Her daughter was halfway across the world. She was having her first, real adventure. Lisa would probably be the furthest thing from her mind for at least the first week. She knew it. But it still hurt.

"And your child isn't with you right now. So what does he want?"

What he wanted was to know if she had made it to the island safely. He knew how long of a drive it was. He also knew that she and Rachel, much as they did try to keep in touch, had a way of getting on each other's nerves when their differences shone, which was often. At their dinner just last night, where they'd together cheered to Maisie's summer experience, Steve had been his usual, kind, jovial self, taking interest in her decision to come back to the island, given that he knew the history.

It was why it was so easy to discuss this with him—because she didn't have to explain anything.

But it was also why it was better to be away. Because all last night, she felt a strange shift in their once comfortable dynamic. A feeling that something had changed. That she'd been replaced. That Steve was leaving her.

Again.

It was silly. Pathetic, really. They were divorced.

"Oh, parenting stuff," Lisa said to Ashley, walking over to the fridge and then remembering that they hadn't been shopping yet, so nothing would be inside. Still, for lack of wanting to turn around and face her youngest sister, who was still standing patiently at the sink, she pulled open the door, happy to see that at least the interior light still functioned. The wine bottles her sister had brought in her luggage rested on the top rack. A quick check of the freezer revealed filled ice-cube trays, too.

Her phone pinged again. Startled, she slammed the fridge door closed. Across the kitchen, Ashley was watching her with a pointed look.

"Steve again?"

"We're friends, Ashley. We're mature adults. Relationships are complicated. Besides, divorce doesn't always make people enemies," she said, regretting her words when she saw the shadow that fell over her sister's face.

Ashley flicked off the tap and with two hands, heaved the pot onto the stovetop, and flicked on the burner. "Guess I wouldn't know," she said, with a shrug, all cheerfulness restored when she turned back to the room.

"Still haven't found anyone special yet?"

Ashley gave her a funny look. "Still not looking for anyone special is more like it."

Lisa looked at her sister frankly. Ashley had always proclaimed she had no interest in getting married, even when she was just a teenager. It had saddened Lisa at first, realizing the impact that their parents' divorce must have had on her, as the youngest, still living under their roof. Now, so many years later, she thought she sensed some hesitation in her sister.

But she wouldn't push it. Not tonight. Tonight was the first night back on the island and the first time the three of them were reunited in years, much less in this house. She intended to make it a nice time and forget about all the other things that were bothering her.

"I'll set up the table on the front porch," she said, grabbing some of the plates from the cabinet nearest the farmhouse table, grinning that some part of her had remembered where they were. The pattern was different than she remembered it, though. Faded with time, the roses along the edge were smaller than she'd pictured them as a child, less vibrant, more dull.

Time was a funny thing, she thought as she carried them down the hall, past the rooms she hadn't gone back into yet but would, tomorrow. It distorted the good times and the bad, muddling everything in between.

But this house was only full of good times. And that was how they would leave it.

Once she was alone on the front porch, she sank into a wicker chair, admiring the view and gripping her cell phone. She'd only been eighteen when she'd met Steve. Twenty when she'd married him, and only because of Maisie. At least, only then because of Maisie. Neither of them had been prepared for the responsibility of parenthood, the realities of adult life, and all the struggles that came with it. How many times had they argued over what their life might have been if they hadn't ended up in that situation? Would they have stayed together, and eventually started a family at a time when they were more prepared? Or would they have found they weren't a good fit, after all, broken up for other reasons, and ended up with different people?

Lisa swallowed hard, her eyes falling on a sailboat gliding across the water at an impressive speed. The breeze was picking up and she shivered, rubbing at her skin, knowing she should dash inside and grab a cardigan. And she would. Just not yet.

She pulled up the screen, reading back over Steve's texts, wondering why it mattered to her that he cared enough to ask if she'd made it safe when he had gone on a date just two nights ago. And it might not have even been the first—just the first she knew about.

She should ignore it. Set the boundaries that Rachel had been telling her to do for years. Use this time to create the distance she needed to move on as he had.

She chewed her lip, starting a text and then erasing it, finally deciding that she would be brief, tell him she had talked to Maisie, that she would be busy, that she would be back in touch when she returned—when Maisie returned. She crafted the text, keeping it breezy, focused on their shared responsibility, the wonderful girl who had brought them together, and maybe even kept them together, long after they'd called it quits.

Maisie, who had probably already checked in with her father, who wouldn't need her mother doing it for her.

Lisa's finger hovered over the button, and with a silent scolding at herself, she tapped it quickly.

A warning flashed on the screen. No service. Unable to send.

With shaking hands, she stood and walked to the door in search of that cardigan. It was just as well, she told herself. She was here to say goodbye to her past for good. And Steve was a part of it.

8
RACHEL

Rachel sat on the edge of what she used to call her summer bed, taking in the familiar surroundings, from the faded floral quilt to the window ledge with the view of the lake if you stood at just the right angle and tipped your head to the left. Their parents had the front room, the best room, of course, that took up the width of the house with tall windows that made you feel like you could practically step outside and fall into the water below. Now, it seemed almost silly to reserve it rather than let one of them enjoy it. What sense was there in holding on to traditions at this point?

What point, indeed? she thought, looking down at the simple band on her left hand. She and Marty had been far too practical to spend a small fortune on a piece of jewelry, using the money instead toward a down payment on their apartment in one of the best co-op buildings in their neighborhood. One that probably wouldn't like the sound of a baby wailing late into the night.

Rachel tugged at the drawer of the bedside table, not

entirely surprised to find that it was empty. Once, it would have held her treasures: special stones from the lakefront, a four-leaf clover from the Morgans' yard, fresh flowers from the Taylors' perennial beds that she pressed between hardback books and then glued onto paper. With renters occupying the house, she supposed that it only made sense to clear out personal artifacts, to eliminate all traces of the family that had once lived here, the people they'd been.

Her skin still felt damp from the shower, which hadn't been exactly warm, and her ring slid down around her knuckle as she moved her hand, drawing her attention to it once more. Pulling her thoughts to Marty, who could be doing anything with anyone at this very moment. He had been very supportive of her coming here for a week, almost suspiciously so. Maybe she should have asked him then and there, gotten her answer before she'd boarded the train for the suburbs, where Lisa was picking her up at the station. But didn't she already have it?

Firming her mouth, she swiftly, almost all too easily, pulled the ring from her finger and dropped it into the empty drawer, the keeper of special things, of the treasures that cumulated her life. A single ring of gold. Really, she didn't know why her finger should feel so bare without it!

Her stomach stirred with unease and she closed the drawer with more force than she intended and stood, feeling restless but not quite ready to go downstairs yet. Facing her sisters meant putting on her game face, one that she wore more often than she admitted to herself. How many times had she felt too tired to want to schmooze at another charity event, to put on yet another pair of heels, make small talk, and stay out later than she preferred? How many times had she tried to keep up her interest in another work dinner, with a couple she couldn't connect with, after a long day of already listening to other people?

How often did she share her own problems, rather than listen to everyone else's?

Never. It was a very easy answer. And a deliberate choice.

Now, though, as she stared at the pages of the draft of the book she had been writing for the better part of the last two years, she wondered how she could ever bring herself to finish it. She was a so-called expert in helping other people. And she couldn't even help herself.

Rachel shoved the papers in the top drawer of the desk and crossed to the nearest window, attempting to fling it open but resulting in more of a tug. The house was well over a hundred years old, and the wood swelled with the heat. With a grunt, she managed to lift it five inches, knowing that she'd probably have to leave it that way, at least until it rained.

But it never rained for long here on Evening Island, not during these summer months. Here, the sun shone, the sky often a true blue against the lush green foliage. It was the one place on earth that Rachel could always guarantee to be bright.

And that was why she'd come. It wasn't about saying goodbye to this house or even spending time with her sisters. She put on her running shoes and clocked five miles every morning. But today, she'd actually run away.

The sound of her sisters' voices trailed up from the porch that wrapped around the side of the house. Feeling like a kid again, she bent down and stuck her face against the open part of the window. "Hey, don't eat all the food without me!"

"Hurry up and get your butt down here or I just might!" came Ashley's distinct holler.

And just for a moment, it really was like no time had passed at all.

* * *

Dinner was always on the porch growing up. Lunch, too. Even snacks. While the girls of West End Road spent their days pedaling bikes, grabbing their towels and crossing the road to the lakefront or exploring the woods for wild berries, the three mothers of the neighboring homes would sit on the porches, drinking iced tea which probably later turned to wine, playing cards, and often laughing until the sun went down. It was one of the reasons that Rachel always slept with the window cracked. She loved the peal of her mother's laugh. It was a sound that was rarely heard at home, or on the weekends when their father came to the island after a long week of work. At some point, summers became the only time that Rachel could remember seeing her mother so relaxed and happy.

"Penny for your thoughts," Lisa said, as she twirled her spaghetti.

Rachel pulled her attention from the lake with a sigh. It was late in the evening by now and the air had turned cooler. All the sisters were draped in the threadbare throw blankets their mother had always stocked in the upstairs linen closet, but none of them showed any interest in going back inside.

"I was just thinking how happy Mom always was here," she said. Then, hesitating, she asked, "How did she react to you telling her you intended to list the house?"

Lisa refilled their glasses. "You know how she is. Any mention of our life before the divorce and she gets all nervous and changes the subject. I heard all about Roberto's new sailboat, though."

Ashley snorted into her wineglass. "Yep, that sounds like her. I like Roberto, though. I hope he lasts."

Rachel knew that Roberto, like the many men who had come before him, would not last past Christmas, but didn't say that. Instead, her curiosity was piqued. "When did you meet Roberto?"

Ashley's blush was obvious even in the dusk. "Oh. I was down there for a wedding in the spring, so I saw Mom for a few days."

"It's okay, Ashley, you don't need to feel guilty for seeing her," Lisa said, even though it was clear that she did. Lisa had already been in college when the divorce happened, Rachel her senior year of high school, and for many years Ashley had stayed behind, keeping their mother company.

If anyone should feel guilty, Rachel thought, it should be her and Lisa. But then, Lisa had a new husband and baby of her own. A new family.

What excuse did Rachel have? Her studies, she supposed. Her perfect academic record. Her ambitious career path.

Her power couple status.

"How did she seem?" Rachel asked tightly. Beside her, she could see that Lisa had stopped eating as she waited for the response.

After a beat, Ashley brushed a hand through the air. "Oh, you know Mom. She's blissfully happy."

"For now." Rachel gritted her teeth the moment she blurted it out, cursing silently to herself when she saw Ashley's stricken expression. She was a grown adult now, but still a child in so many ways. So full of hope where none should exist. For years, she had indulged in a fantasy of their parents getting back together. At least she'd finally let go of that dream. Maybe Dad's third wife had finally convinced her.

"Sorry," Rachel said, holding up a hand. "I don't mean to sound cynical. I want Mom to be happy, too."

"It's just too bad that she's depending on a man to find it," Ashley said, resulting in a surprised glance from Lisa.

"Now who sounds cynical?" Rachel said with a laugh. "I hope you don't tell your blog readers that."

Ashley rolled her eyes. "Very funny. The blog is going very well. The only problem is that I'm running out of weddings to attend. I might have to start making new friends. Unless...?" She glanced at Lisa hopefully, who was a little slow on the uptake.

"What?" Lisa asked, through a mouthful of food. "Gosh, no!"

"But you're only thirty-five," Ashley pointed out.

"And I feel like I'm forty-five," Lisa replied.

Rachel shook her head. "And that's just the problem. Look at you. You could get out there again, meet someone new."

"Have more children, even," Ashley added.

Rachel took a long sip of her wine. Talking about hypothetical futures was not her idea of fun. Certainty was always better.

"And what about you?" Lisa said, turning the attention back to Ashley. Clearly, she shared Rachel's sentiments. "You're young and beautiful. Is there anyone special in your life?"

"Oh, no. No." Ashley shook her head firmly.

"You mean you're going to all these weddings solo? Sitting at the singles table?" Rachel could think of little worse than sitting with a group of strangers—well, other than her husband cheating on her. "There must be plenty of guys in Manhattan to date."

"I don't sit at the singles table," Ashley corrected. "I sit at the head table. I'm always in the wedding party. Besides, I'm so busy tending to the bride, I wouldn't have time to dance."

The way she evaded eye contact made Rachel think that there was more she wasn't sharing. Ashley had always been an earnest girl, even as a child still in pigtails, always eager to help, to be included in anything the older girls were doing. Now, Rachel felt a pang in her chest when she realized that it had been a long time since she'd brought her little sister into the fold. An even longer time since Ashley had stopped asking.

"You made a lot of good friends at that sorority," she noted, hoping that her tone didn't match the resentment that sometimes lingered over this. After all, she had her career, and Marty: why shouldn't Ashley have her own life too?

"Dozens!" Ashley beamed. "And I've now been to dozens of weddings!"

"Next there will be dozens of baby showers," Lisa said brightly. "Hey, maybe you can switch gears, or grow your blog that way."

Right. Because of course, that was the normal course of things, right. Marriage, then babies. Except that wasn't what she and Marty had agreed to. Or wanted.

Now, she wondered if that had been the problem all along. If the two of them weren't enough to keep them together.

"Maybe," Ashley said, noncommittally. She frowned down at her plate for a moment, and then pushed it away.

"Well," Lisa said, standing to gather up the plates. "I think I'll get to bed. It's been a long drive and I have a lot of work to do tomorrow to get this place ready to list. And you have a lot of work to do on that book of yours, right?"

Rachel startled, realizing that Lisa was staring at her.

Marty. The book. So much for not thinking of all the aspects of her life that up until a week ago had been a given, not a growing uncertainty.

"You know, I think it's only fair that I help with the house too," she said. "The book can wait."

It would have to. Until she figured out how she could finish it. If she could even finish it.

Lisa looked surprised but pleased. "You sure?"

"Very."

"Between your organizational skills and Lisa's decorative flair, this place might end up looking better than ever!" Ashley said.

Rachel doubted that, but it was true that together, they would be able to make some stride.

"Well, the sooner we get it fixed up, the sooner we can sell it!" Lisa grinned broadly and then disappeared through the screen door.

Rachel narrowed her eyes long after her sister had gone into the house. She wondered now why Lisa was so eager to suddenly get this house sold.

And why she wouldn't mind if it dragged out all summer.

9
ASHLEY

The Morgan family, like the Taylors and the Andersons, was comprised of three daughters, all close enough in age that the nine children played together all summer long, always reuniting each June as if no time had passed.

But now, sixteen years had passed, and as Ashley and Lisa made the trek across the lawn the next morning to the large Victorian home affectionately called Sunset Cottage, she felt a strange ripple of apprehension.

So much of their time here on the island was tucked away, in a safe place, nearly as literally as the box of photos and mementos that she carried with her from college to her apartment, to her next apartment, always to be set high up on a shelf in a closet, but never opened.

"Do you think Gemma will even remember us?" she asked Lisa a little nervously as they took the steps to the porch.

"Of course she will!" Lisa grinned. "I just hope she forgives us for losing touch."

"It happens," Ashley said. After all, it had happened even with them. Outside of an annual Christmas card, she wouldn't have even known how much her own niece had grown over the years. She knew the bare basics, gleaned from her mother, or from her once or twice annual call with either Lisa or Rachel, but she didn't know the details of her sisters' lives.

And they didn't know hers. And somewhere over time, she'd learned to prefer it that way. Besides, if last night was any hint of how future conversations would go, it was definitely for the best. The last thing she needed was to have one of them pushing her toward a way of life that she'd chosen to run from instead.

"Do you think she'll even hear a knock?" Ashley felt doubtful as she tipped her head back and took in the large home, knowing just how many rooms and corners the structure contained. If Gemma was still writing—which, Lisa had informed her this morning she was, and published, too—then she was likely tucked up in that top-floor room with the window overlooking the lake, from a bird's eye view. They'd probably have a better chance of getting her attention by standing on the grass and shouting up to her. Or attempting to climb the rose trellis, which she and Gemma's younger sister Ellie had done exactly once, before ending up at the Island Hospital for minor scrapes and luckily no stitches.

"Remember how we used to just let ourselves in?" Lisa grinned as she knocked, loudly, on the wooden door and then pressed her nose closer to the glass pane. "She's coming!"

For some reason, Ashley's heart began to pound. But any

of the nerves she'd felt were quieted when the door flung open and a smiling woman with tousled brown hair squealed their names and widened her arms.

"I can't believe you're both here! Word in town was that just Lisa was making the trip." Gemma's eyes glimmered when she stared at Ashley. "You're all grown up! But then, Ellie is, too. She'll be back by next week, if you're still here then?"

Ashley glanced at Lisa. She knew that Lisa was planning to remain here until the house was ready (or until Maisie returned from Europe) but her own plans had no end date. She hadn't made much decision beyond packing her bags and booking a flight to the nearest airport, and even that task had felt enormous.

"Maybe?" She gave a noncommittal shrug.

"More like hopefully," Gemma said, grinning devilishly. "You know that the Taylors were all back last summer. Now Heather and Andrea are both living on the island. But that's a long story for a proper visit."

"Wow. It's like a real reunion," Lisa said, looking a little taken aback.

Ashley echoed her thoughts. All this time, they'd never visited, while their dearest childhood friends had made this island their home. A pang of something she recognized as jealousy tightened in her stomach.

"And it only took how many years?" Gemma waggled her eyebrows. "I only wish we'd kept in better touch. I never saw the Taylors the entire time I lived in Chicago."

"Me neither," Lisa said, looking as regretful as Ashley

felt, even though, in fairness, Ashley had not lived in Chicago since she'd left for college. She might have returned more often—if her parents hadn't sold the Lake Shore Drive apartment and split the assets. One day she'd arrived back at her dorm to discover a stack of boxes containing her neatly packed childhood belongings. She'd gone to her roommate's suburban Connecticut home for Christmas that year. And another's for summer break. She'd made it a point to pledge the sorority that fall. To replace the home she'd lost.

"It's different in the city," Gemma went on, seeming to hold no ill will, only partial responsibility. "There was something about this place that brought us all together. In a way, it was nice to keep it that way."

"And now half of us are together again!" Lisa glanced around. "Although I can see your home is in much better shape."

"Oh, it wasn't when I first came back, even though Ellie had been here looking after our grandmother..." Gemma's eyes widened. "But that's a story for another day. I'm going to invite you all to dinner, this Saturday when Ellie's back. I'm guessing right now you're hoping to talk to Leo."

"The sooner we can get that house fixed up the better," Lisa said, nodding. "I know he's more familiar with it in recent years than I am."

"Of course. The rental rates must be nice," Gemma said.

Ashley shifted her gaze to her sister, but Lisa didn't correct their friend. Instead, she said, "We know that Leo doesn't do that type of work anymore, but I thought he might have a list of things he could suggest we tackle?"

"You're right that he's hung up his hammer, well, except when I beg and plead," Gemma laughed. "But you can probably find him in town. He's got a small law office, just off Main, near the harbor. You can't miss it."

Lisa nodded. "I'll go over now. I hate to stop by and run."

"Please," Gemma said, swiping a hand through the air. "That's what's so great about the island. We were always in and out of each other's homes. It wouldn't feel right otherwise. Maybe we can all grab a drink in town? Tomorrow night?"

Ashley and Lisa both nodded. "We'll bring Rachel too."

"Rachel!" Gemma's smile was radiant. Growing up, she'd been closest in age to Ashley's middle sister, while Lisa was closest with Gemma's older sister, Hope.

"She had some work to do. You know she's a licensed therapist." Ashley perked up on a thought. "And she's writing her first book. Self-help, not fiction, but she'll probably want to tell you all about it herself."

"I can't wait to hear all your news!" Gemma sighed. "You sure I can't offer you both a lemonade or some iced tea?"

Lisa grinned. "Later, for sure. I'll...feel better once I get some movement on that house."

Ashley was still watching her sister as they took the steps back down to the lawn a moment later. For someone who hadn't shown must interest in the house for over a dozen years, Lisa seemed strangely fixated on it. Why the urgency to sell, and why now?

And why, as they began the descent into town, did Lisa keep checking her phone for cell coverage?

* * *

Ashley left Lisa at the edge of town, deciding to tag team their errands, but also because she didn't see how much use she could be to her sister right now. Lisa had a vision, one that seemed to include a lot of dollar signs; Ashley wasn't exactly known for putting much care into her dwellings. Her apartment in New York was a studio with a mini-fridge and a hot plate. She didn't mind because she was rarely in it other than to sleep or shower, and even then, she usually freshened up at the gym. She didn't see much point in getting attached to a piece of property—not when it could so easily be taken away.

"I'll get us some groceries," she promised, noticing her sister's doubtful look. "I can easily handle four bags on my own. I'm a New Yorker," she reminded her.

Lisa frowned and opened her mouth to say something but then stopped herself. "I suppose you are. I guess I still haven't ever gotten used to the thought that you've made a life for yourself so far away."

"Didn't have much choice, did I?" Ashley shrugged. "Besides, I like to cook. I don't get a chance to do it enough back at my apartment. I use my oven as a shoe closet."

Lisa laughed. "Okay, then. Meet you back at the house later?"

Ashley nodded and turned to walk in the other direction, surprised that she even remembered where the grocery was, and hoping that it actually was still there when she reached the corner. There was a strange relief in being alone again, even though she didn't exactly mind her sisters' company. It was more that she didn't know how to be around them anymore. And every conversation felt both stiff and far too emotional at once when she longed for easy banter and casual interactions.

Main Street was lined with shops of all varieties, most of which had been here since she was a little girl and generations beyond that. She slowed her pace to let a couple on a tandem bicycle scoot around a particularly slow-moving horse and buggy and stopped to watch two candy makers turning fudge on a marble countertop through the window of a candy store. The smell was sweet and rich and wafted after her as she moved on, past the various boutiques selling art prints and home goods until she was all but forced to go back for it.

The bell on the door jingled her arrival and she marched over to the beautiful walnut display case and studied her options, calculating how much she would eat on the walk home and how much she should buy so there was some left over for her sisters.

"I'll do the mixed box of six," she said, realizing once the shopgirl handed it over to her that she'd probably overestimated her ability to consume it all. But there was Gemma to share it with, and maybe Ellie, too. And the Taylors.

She was smiling as she paid for the purchase, and already stuffing a piece of raspberry dark-chocolate-flavored fudge into her mouth by the time she walked back onto the sidewalk—and straight into the wall of something warm and hard.

"Oh!" She backed up, still clutching the fudge in her

hand, looking up into the face of a guy in his early thirties, with dark brown hair and handsome features. From the amused glint in the man's eyes, she realized that she might have smeared a little fudge on her face when they collided.

"Sorry about that," he said good-naturedly.

"I didn't expect so much traffic on the sidewalk for a Monday," Ashley replied. She was holding the bag containing the box of fudge in one hand, and she stared at the hunk of fudge in the other, wondering if she should attempt to try to wipe at her mouth or just finish eating first.

The guy seemed to note her inner struggle as he fought off a grin rather than move on with his day, as she'd expect him to.

With a sigh, Ashley shoved the rest of the fudge into her mouth and chewed. It was warm and sticky and darn it if it didn't seem to take just about a minute shy of forever to get it down.

Finally, the man's face broke out into a grin. "You have a little something." He gestured to his upper lip.

She wiped at the same spot. He gestured again. She tried again.

"Here," he said, gingerly lifting his hand to her face. He rubbed the pad of his thumb over the top of her lip and then grinned. "There."

"Thanks," Ashley said, feeling a blush creep up her cheeks.

"First time on the island?" he asked, as if aggressive fudge consumption was reserved for newbies.

Ashley hesitated. It would be easy to pretend that was

exactly the case. She could have him show her around, maybe they'd rent a pair of bikes, and do a lap of the island while he pointed out all the best spots that only the locals knew about. It would be a nice way to spend the day when she thought about it, and she might have done just that if she were still back in New York, where the odds of running into him again were slim, if not nonexistent. But this was Evening Island. She knew the Morgans and the Taylors, who were both back in town, and, of course, about half the other locals who would no doubt recognize her before she'd pedaled past the old church steeple before the first bend.

"I'm what you'd call a summer person," Ashley said without much enthusiasm. "Or I used to be, at least. My family has a house here, but I haven't been back in a while."

"Shame." His eyes glimmered in a way that might make some girls swoon, but only made her flutter. A little.

She knew the type. He was all about a good time. He liked the fun of it: the flirtation, the dance, the thrill of that first kiss. She knew because she was the same way. And he probably knew it, too.

"You live here?" She didn't know why she was surprised, other than she didn't recognize him. But then, why should she? It had been over a dozen years since she'd been back here, and even though the house and the buildings hadn't changed much in her absence, people had moved on, just like her.

"I do," he said with a proud nod. "Took over a bar a while back."

"Business must be booming then," she said, knowing that the many restaurants and watering holes made the most of the summer months and then often closed down for the winter when the ferry stopped running.

"I can't complain," he said easily. His gaze held hers long enough for her heart to speed up a bit, pulling her back to reality.

"Well, I should get going. I promised my sister I'd pick up some food, and if I don't make good on my promise, no one will have any lunch."

"And here I was just about to suggest that I buy you lunch." The broad grin with the straight white teeth flashed.

She bit back a smile as she stood, albeit a little reluctantly. "It'll have to be another time."

"How long are you on the island for?"

Ashley thought back to her earlier uncertainty and gave him a slow smile in response before turning and walking away, knowing that she'd see him again because the island was small like that.

A watercolor painting in a shop window caught her eye —one of West End Road—the three houses all facing the water, the shrubs flowering in full glory. It was signed, she noticed with pride—by Ellie Morgan. Her heart beat faster as she leaned in, noticing another one signed by her friend. This one of Main Street, taken at Christmastime. The roads were covered in snow, a horse and buggy were parked out front of one of the inns, and a sparkling tree took center stage. Even though there were no people in the painting, the sense of community was so real, so vivid, that Ashley felt a longing for the very place she now was.

A longing she'd denied for so, so long.

Finally deciding it was time to move on, or crash into yet

another pedestrian, she backed away from the window to see the man still sitting on the bench, grinning at her.

She smiled back and then moved toward the market, thinking that maybe she should stick around town long enough to see her old friend Ellie again.

That suddenly, this trip looked a little more interesting.

10
LISA

After her brief meeting with Leo Helms, and armed with a considerably long list of issues at the house ranging from small to mildly scary, Lisa could understand how the man had won Gemma's heart.

"Gemma mentioned something about a dinner party," she said before she left. "This weekend."

Leo, a tall, fit man with a great smile and kind eyes, grinned. "Perfect. It will give me a chance to get to know you all better. So far, all I've heard were the stories from your youth."

"Oh, I can only imagine the opinions you've formed then," she said, laughing, but something nagged at her. Leo seemed like a good, solid guy, and someone she would normally like to get to know better, especially considering that he was engaged to Gemma. But after this visit, she'd never see him again. Or Gemma, for that matter.

"Enviable ones," he said, his eyes glimmering. "You all had idyllic summers."

Lisa felt like she'd been hit straight through the chest. "We did," she said, a little breathlessly. And it was a shame that they'd had to stop. Worse, that they'd been purposefully forgotten.

She waved her list in the air. "Thanks again for this."

"My pleasure. Most of it is normal wear and tear. Nothing a little pain and some TLC can't fix. I'm sure the house is happy to have its family back to tend to it."

Lisa's smile slipped further. "Yes, well, judging from the length of the list, I'll certainly be busy!"

She left through the door, and looked left and then right, unsure which direction she wanted to go, even though she knew where each path would lead her. The one place she wasn't ready to return to just yet was the house, even if it was her purpose for being here.

It was late morning, and she'd skipped breakfast. Up ahead, she saw the Island Bakery, grinning when she thought of how much they'd always enjoyed the pies, usually on the porch, Ashley often staining her fingers in the process from the berries.

Inside, the line was long, even for a Monday, when most of the tourists would have left to go back to the mainland, or the Midwest cities that they lived and worked in. Still, it was summertime, and there were people who would come for a week, or, like the Andersons, for the entire summer at one point.

"Lisa?" a voice cut through the bustle of the bakery, forcing Lisa to glance over her shoulder. "Lisa Anderson! I thought that was you!"

Lisa felt her smile whither as the woman she recognized

as Sally Hayworth approached, showing little apology for cutting the line ahead of two teenage girls and a young couple linking hands. Sally lived on the island year-round and felt she deserved special treatment as a result.

"Why, it's been years! But I would recognize you anywhere! And, it helps that I happened to see Leo the other day and he mentioned that you were coming to town. Not that you've changed a bit in all these years. No one else has those big, beautiful, brown eyes."

Lisa couldn't help but flush at the compliment, maybe because they were so few and far between these days, or maybe because she'd been feeling a little doubtful ever since learning about Steve's new love life. Maisie was at a phase where she cared about following the latest trends, and she wasn't shy in pointing out if something made Lisa look too old or—possibly worse—too young. Lisa had to often refrain from pointing out that, considering how young she'd been when she had Maisie, she was young compared to the mothers of her daughter's friends.

"It's so nice to see you again, Sally," Lisa said, realizing that she meant it. Growing up, she loved knowing that she would see the same people summer after summer, that while the kids continued to grow and mature, the adults all stayed the same, like how the house always looked in June exactly as it did when they closed the door behind them every August. It was a constant, a guarantee.

Now it seemed almost impossible to believe that anything in life had ever felt certain.

"Are you still at the newspaper?" she asked the older woman now.

"Of course! And so is Heather Taylor, but you must already know that. But I'm not here to gossip," Sally said quickly.

Lisa suppressed a smile and inched up in line. "Yes, I hear that Gemma and Heather and Andrea are all on the island."

"Such a shame about Mrs. Taylor," Sally said, shaking her head. "But then, you heard?"

Lisa blinked. She hadn't heard. She was ashamed to admit how little she'd kept up with the island news...or the people.

"Passed away. Years ago."

Lisa, who hadn't really thought of Mrs. Taylor in years, felt her eyes mist. She swallowed hard, blinking back the tears before they fell, thinking that she really had no right to be so upset by this news, except that she was. Somewhere, deep inside her, she'd always dared to believe that this island was still exactly like she'd left it.

"And what brings you back at long last?" Sally asked, shifting topics rather urgently before motioning for Lisa to scoot up in line.

"Oh, just fixing up the house. We no longer have a caretaker, with Edward retiring and Leo focusing on his law profession. He's been nice enough to still help out a little last year but...it was time."

"High time!" Sally clucked her disappointment. "Can't imagine not returning to the island for so many years! But then, last I knew, you were starting a family."

Lisa felt her smile wane. Yes, it was right around the time of their last summer here that she'd met Steve. Back then, her future had felt so bright, and when she pictured herself at the age she was now, she assumed Steve would still be at her side.

And he was. Just not in the way she'd hoped.

"I have a daughter now," she told Sally. "Maisie is fifteen. She's actually doing a summer abroad program."

"And she's never been to the island!" Now Sally made a show of narrowing her eyes and shaking her head, making Lisa feel a sense of regret that hadn't been there before.

Yes, it was a travesty, but it wasn't exactly so simple, was it? For so many years, this house, the island, and all its memories were tainted. The laughter and lightness that she'd once associated with it were overshadowed by everything that had happened that last summer they were still technically a family. The summer coming to an abrupt end when their mother learned what their father was up to back in Chicago. Rachel never wanted to describe it, but Ashley had called Lisa at school, crying. Every night for a month.

Now Lisa wondered when Ashley had stopped reaching out to her for comfort. And why.

"Well, now that you're back, maybe next time you'll bring that lovely daughter of yours."

Lisa smiled, but there was a heaviness in her chest when she considered that it was too late now—that Maisie would never see this island, much less understand the simple joys that were so different from the bustle of their regular lives. That the house wouldn't be passed down to her. That long before that decision had been made, Lisa had decided not to pass down the tradition of these summers.

"And how is your mother?" Sally asked, giving her a peering look that told Lisa that there had been talk about their family situation, speculation no doubt that grew with their absence over the years.

"I don't talk to her much," Lisa said tactfully, knowing that was even more deceiving than pretending she was not the product of two broken homes. Her conversations with her mother were limited to once a year at best, sometimes just a message on Christmas day. Like the house was to her and her sisters, so Lisa's mother's daughters were to her. A reminder of another family, a happier one. Another life. One that had been snatched out from under her. Or maybe, Lisa thought, thinking of Ashley's tears and Rachel's stiff upper lip, given away.

"Well, next time you do, send her all our love from the island. And tell her that she's missed at the gardening club. You know how involved she was with the annual festival effort."

"I will," Lisa promised. She was a little relieved when Sally gave a jump and said she just remembered she had an interview with a local author. She gave Lisa's arm a squeeze and scooted back out of the bakery, leaving the teenage girls behind Lisa to scoot up into her place with a sense of propriety.

Approaching the counter, Lisa ordered an iced coffee and a blueberry corn muffin and then, on a whim, said, "And the mixed berry pie. With the crumble topping." She wondered idly if Ashley would have bought ice cream at the grocery store. Probably not, given that it could melt by the time she made it back to the house but that was fine. Just the thought of sitting on the porch, letting the time linger into dessert, felt like a treat.

And it definitely beat sitting around her empty house back in Chicago, wondering and worrying about Maisie.

Or Steve and his new girlfriend.

The girl behind the counter handed over the signature blue bakery bag that held the pie box and the muffin, and swiped Lisa's credit card. For the first time since getting in the car yesterday morning, Lisa felt a prickle of panic. She'd been relying on the credit card more and more lately, and each time she did, she was almost afraid to look at the balance. It was so unlike her, and maybe, that should be her wake-up call. To find a new career. Give up on the gift shop.

Or sell that house on West End Road.

The girl handed back the card with a smile. "Have a nice day!"

Lisa nearly wept with relief as she tucked it back firmly into her wallet. "You too," she said and pushed back out the door into the sunshine.

She settled on a bench near the waterfront, telling herself that she'd eat her food and watch the boats on the water, but she was close to one of the bigger inns in town, and her mind traveled, wondering idly if she had decent service right about now. It would be evening by now in France. Maisie would probably be getting ready for dinner. Or maybe sleeping off the jet lag. She should leave her alone, send one text at the most really, and assume that no news was good news instead of worrying about the hundred things that could have gone wrong or happened to her daughter, while she was none the wiser.

Decision made, she pulled out her phone, cringing only

slightly when her fingers pushed aside the list from Leo. Three bars. That would be enough.

Three bars and no messages from Maisie, though.

There was, however, a new text from Steve.

She chewed a nail, and then, reminding herself of the vision of Steve sitting at the dimly lit bistro, with a faceless companion that for some reason Lisa assumed would be blond, because she would have to be, right? She would be the opposite of Lisa in every way: blond instead of brunette, with blue eyes instead of brown. She'd be taller than Lisa's average height. Thinner too, of course.

Feeling sick at the thought and angry at herself for caring, Lisa shuffled through her bag again and found the list. It was long and detailed, but most of it she could tackle herself. When she and Steve had bought their house, now her house, it had been a fixer-upper, the only thing they could afford at the time and even then it had been a stretch. Together they'd learned how to properly sand and paint and edge, how to tend to a garden, how to fix old window sashes and loose knobs, even some simple wiring, not that she'd dare touch anything at the lake house—no, this house was far too old.

Pushing away any wistful memories of her better times with Steve before she became nostalgic and clouded her judgment, she forced her attention back to her list. She'd need to buy supplies and tap into the house fund account—something that she managed but never tapped into personally. Out went the money for the property manager or caretaker, and in came the money for the rent. Like her credit card statements, she didn't check the balance, but in this case, she didn't need to. The house until now had been a distant issue, something that she only ever thought about come the springtime, something that seemed so far removed from her regular life that it sometimes came as a surprise when the caretaker even checked in with her when the harsh Michigan winter had come to an end and the grass had started to sprout.

Now, though, the house deserved her attention, and she would give it some. Because it sure as heck beat giving that energy to Steve, who was starting the next phase of his life, just like Rachel had been urging her to do.

Well, this time she was finally going to listen to her sister's advice.

11
RACHEL

The knock on the door came only minutes after Rachel was regretting her choice not to join her sisters for an afternoon walk along the shoreline. She'd used the same excuse as this morning, when she couldn't bring herself to go into town, claiming that she had to work on her book, even though she wasn't sure that she'd ever be able to write another word in it.

Who was she to be giving out advice, when she couldn't even help herself?

Happy for the distraction from her darkening thoughts, she hurried down the steps, her mood picking up when she saw the familiar figure through the frosted glass pane.

"Gemma!"

Opposed to her own more reserved nature, Gemma wasted no time in pulling her in for a long, hard hug the moment that Rachel pulled open the heavy door. It was only once Rachel allowed herself to relax into the warm embrace that she realized just how long it had been since she'd been properly held like that.

Marty, like herself, was more of a minimalist when it came to affection, especially in public. They greeted each other with a perfunctory kiss when he returned home from his business trips. They never held hands. But now, seeing how easy it was for Gemma to show such warmth, Rachel felt stiff in comparison.

Was that the reason he had strayed? Had he secretly longed for something more than they shared? More than she was capable of giving him?

She tucked those thoughts away for another day or a long night. She wasn't getting much sleep these days, though the cool lake breeze that drifted through her window last night had helped. A bit.

"I'm not interrupting anything, am I?"

Rachel smiled at her old friend, who still looked as fresh-faced and carefree as she had all those years back, still sporting a peasant blouse and cut-off jean shorts, her bare feet tucked into aging leather flip-flops.

By comparison, Rachel felt overdressed. In her linen capris and crisp white tank, she was better suited for an afternoon drink on Oak Street around the corner from her co-op building rather than some lemonade on the porch of this oversized and slightly rundown home on a remote island.

Deciding to stay barefoot, she said, "Ashley went to the store earlier, so I could make us some iced tea?"

She frowned slightly, as a memory came back to her. One of her helping her mother with what they liked to call "sun tea" because they left it to brew out on the back patio all afternoon. Her mother and Gemma's mother would go through a gallon of that a day, and then start the ritual all over the next morning.

But Rachel didn't have that kind of time. She could make a cup of tea the regular way and then cool it down with ice.

"No need," Gemma said, pointing to a pitcher of lemonade on the table in the wicker seating area. "All we need are the glasses."

While Gemma settled onto the porch, Rachel hurried back to the kitchen, where she grabbed two of the glasses etched with fading flowers and eyed the bowl of fruit on the counter. She hadn't eaten lunch, even when Ashley returned from town and offered to make her a sandwich. She was too busy staring at her notes. Too busy replaying every minute of her relationship with Marty. Too busy feeling like a giant fraud.

She glanced at the pie box that was resting on the counter. While it would be nice to offer it to Gemma, she was sure that Lisa was saving it for dinner tonight.

Her sisters were making an effort, she realized with a twinge of shame. While she'd been hiding from them all day. Vowing to try harder tonight, she decided that company was really the best distraction. Being alone never suited her well, and already her mood was brighter at the thought of a friend waiting for her outside.

"Here we are!" she said breezily as she stepped out onto the porch, still barefoot, and only mildly concerned that she might get a splinter. There was always the threat, of course, and it was known to happen. Ashley always seemed to attract them, probably because she ran with the most force, jumping straight into the action as if she couldn't let a moment of life slip her by.

"Oh, these glasses!" Gemma smiled fondly as she took one and studied it for a moment. "I forgot all about these. Each one in the set was different. I always loved the lilacs."

Rachel glanced down at her own glass, which depicted a fading daffodil. Gemma had a rose. "I could trade it out for you?"

Gemma laughed and filled their glasses. "If I was still twelve, I'd probably have you do just that."

Rachel watched as Gemma folded her legs up under her on the chair, making herself at home in a way that even Rachel couldn't quite yet do. The house, by all appearances, was the same. The patio furniture was slightly more weathered, the paint on the siding, too, but otherwise, it was all the same.

And yet, so different.

"I hear that you are a famous author!" Rachel was all too eager to hear about Gemma's life. Lisa had filled them in on everything she'd gleaned from her bits of communication with the islanders over the years, but it wasn't much.

"Well, I'm a published author, though I'm not so sure about famous." Gemma gave a good-natured laugh. "All those rainy days scribbling away paid off, I suppose. Although, I seem to remember you keeping a notebook too."

"A diary," Rachel corrected, surprised that Gemma would remember that when she'd forgotten it herself. "Our mother always made us keep a summer journal. She said she wanted us to remember these summers, but she probably just wanted to give us something to do."

She sipped her lemonade thoughtfully. Then shook the memory away. "I hear you have a boyfriend. Edward's grandson?"

"Leo." At the mention of him, Gemma's face lit up in a way that Rachel couldn't be sure hers ever had. "And he's my fiancé now, actually."

Now, this was news that Lisa hadn't shared. "You're kidding! Congratulations! When's the wedding?"

Gemma laughed. "You sound more excited than me, but thanks. We're thinking of the end of this summer. Something casual. It will depend on when my sisters can all get up here, and my parents."

Rachel loved Gemma the most of her sisters, but she still longed to know more about how the other Morgans had turned out. In her mind, they were still frozen times, girls in their varying teenage years, each with their own interests and passions and dreams for their lives. Now, more than a dozen years had passed. Their futures had happened, their paths determined.

"How's Hope? Ellie?"

"Hope is in Chicago, married, with two adorable girls. And Ellie has been exploring the world recently, focusing on her art. She'll be back this weekend, though. Please tell me you'll still be here and we can have a proper gathering. Andrea Taylor can join us, too. She lives here now. She met a newcomer on the island last summer and fell in love. I don't think she's ever been happier."

"For some reason, I can't imagine Andrea living on Evening Island full-time!" Rachel said. The Andrea she remembered was serious and ambitious. "Wasn't she planning on becoming an architect?"

Gemma nodded. "She was and she is. Now she works for the Historical Society. John, her beau, bought the Lakeside Inn and he's been renovating it. I think he really turned her onto something. There's a way to preserve these properties and keep their integrity. Sort of like these old homes."

Rachel looked up at the porch room and then swept her gaze around to the view. "I don't feel like we've done a great job of taking care of this house, unfortunately."

"Nonsense! You had Edward looking after it. And Leo." Again with the grin. "Anyway, tomorrow night a bunch of us girls are going out. I already mentioned it to Lisa and Ashley. And this weekend, let's definitely have a proper dinner party."

Thinking about this weekend made Rachel start to think about going home, about walking into her apartment, seeing Marty, or not. He'd travel again, or so he would claim to, and she'd go back to work. It would all carry on exactly as it always had, and that was just the problem.

It would all carry on as if this week, and this time on the island, with her sisters and old friends, had never happened.

Rachel pulled in a shaky breath. She didn't want to think about next week. It was too overwhelming. Too uncertain. Her agenda may as well be completely tossed at this point, because every sticker, every plan, was now in question.

"What about Heather? And Kim?" The Andersons had been like cousins, and Gemma and Heather were closest in age to Rachel.

"Kim got married here on the island last summer. And,

are you ready for this?" Gemma leaned in. "Heather just married Billy! They're away on their honeymoon! She'll be so sorry to have missed you."

"Billy Davidson?"

Gemma grinned. "Yup."

"Billy and Heather?" Rachel took a moment to let that sink in. Heather had been in love with Billy since they were too little to even know what love was. Rachel had always thought they'd end up together, but then, like her own relationships with these girls that she thought would never end, the magic tended to fade when they boarded the ferry and watched the island grow small in the distance behind them.

Now, as an adult, it seemed almost impossible that Heather's summer crush had turned out to be something permanent.

"He's a doctor now. Life is funny sometimes," Gemma said, rearranging her legs. "But Heather really followed her heart."

Rachel squirmed in her chair. Normally, this kind of behavior felt reckless, bound for disaster and disappointment. Now, she wondered if she'd gotten it all wrong.

"Now, tell me all about *your* husband," Gemma said. "I want to hear every detail of what you've been up to since we last saw each other, even if it takes all day and night."

Rachel laughed but then realized with a strange twist of embarrassment that the last decade of her life could be summed up in a few sentences.

"I'm a therapist now," she said. "Marital counseling, actually."

She took a sip of the lemonade. It was a warm day and

despite the shade from the porch, her cheeks felt like they were burning.

Talking about herself had never come easily, and now, it made her even more uncomfortable.

"Marty," she said, unable to even say the word "husband" when she wasn't sure that he still would be a week from now, "works in the tech industry. We met after college—he's a few years older than me. We got married about eight years ago. We live in a condo in the heart of the city not far from where I grew up, actually. And...that's about it!"

Gemma tipped her head, giving her a look that said she wasn't buying it. "I can't believe there isn't more to that story!"

Rachel busied herself by refilling her glass, even though she'd only drunk of it. "Boring stuff. Unless you want to hear about some of my patients, though I'd have to keep their names out of it."

Gemma grinned. "Oh, I have my own sordid romantic history that could keep you entertained for hours. Though I'm sure you hear enough about heartache to last a lifetime in your profession."

Rachel nodded. She did. And much as she tried to help each couple work through their problems, it wasn't always in her control.

And that was something that she still struggled to accept.

"And is that what this book you're writing is about?" At Rachel's reaction, she grinned. "Your sisters were bragging about your success when I saw them this morning."

For some reason, the thought of her sisters speaking highly of her made Rachel feel like bursting into tears right then and there. And Rachel didn't cry. She made sure she didn't by never putting herself in a position that could lead to such a reaction. Such emotion.

She realized now that she hadn't cried since discovering that Marty was cheating on her.

And what did that say about her? What would she tell a patient about that?

"It's...an extension of my work," she explained. And it was, and maybe if she remembered that, she could finally finish the draft.

"Well, you're the expert when it comes to a happy marriage!" Gemma said this with no offense, but Rachel felt like she had just been doused with that entire pitcher of icy lemonade.

She wasn't an expert or a success at anything, even if that's what she wanted people to believe. Even if it's what she had wanted to believe. Once.

12
ASHLEY

By seven o'clock the next evening, Ashley was eager for a night out with people other than her sisters. Rachel had spent the majority of the last two days in her bedroom, claiming she was working on her book, which Ashley suspected was just a convenient excuse for not helping Lisa with the house, though. After she'd spent over an hour patching a single nick in the wood trim near the front door and still felt it wasn't quite perfect enough, Lisa had said she'd take over, and Ashley could tell that Lisa was just as relieved as she was to have one less "helper."

Ashley didn't exactly have an excuse, and she didn't mind picking up a paintbrush or a hammer. It gave her something to do, and already in the course of a day they had managed to touch up the trim, patch any damaged spots in the walls, and air out most of the rooms, thanks to the cool evening breezes that the island always promised.

"Think Andrea will be there too?" Ashley asked as they walked down the road. It would have been quicker to bicycle into town, but they hadn't yet tackled the carriage house where their old cruisers were kept. Besides, the climb back up the hill would be painful, especially in the dark and without any streetlamps to guide their way.

"Maybe, but Andrea was never much of the going out for drinks on a weeknight type of person," Lisa said of her old friend.

"But you haven't seen Andrea since before you were old enough to drink," Ashley reminded her.

"Still, people don't really change all that much, do they?" Lisa replied with a shrug.

Ashley glanced at Rachel, to gauge her reaction, but like always, Rachel was quiet, deep in thought. She carried herself with perfect posture, even if she did look a little out of place in that long navy linen shift dress. They were meeting at a pub, for goodness sake! But then, Ashley supposed that Rachel, being married and so devoted to her professional career, hadn't experienced a local joint like this in a long time. If ever.

She grinned, feeling pleased with this thought.

"I guess some things about people don't change, no," she said. Even if so many things did.

The conversation stalled between them as they neared the end of the hill, where the houses grew smaller and closer together, each one painted in a distinct color ranging from turquoise to bright yellow, interspersed by small businesses like the post office, a few gift shops, and small art galleries boasting many of the island's talented artists.

Normally, Ashley would have stopped to see if any of Ellie's work was in the window, but she didn't want to keep

Gemma waiting. She'd promised to secure them a table after an early dinner in town with Leo.

Hackney's was down the next side street, across from a smaller inn, and close to the ice cream shop that was one of the greatest places in the world to Ashley as a kid. Lisa opened the door to the dimly lit but cozy establishment, spotting Gemma immediately, joined by Lena and Mandy, two of the girls whose families went back generations on the island. Mandy had always secured them an extra scoop of ice cream on the hottest days of summer.

"I was just thinking about you!" Ashley hurried to the table to greet her old friends, giving them all a proper squeeze before sliding onto a chair at the head of the table, so she could be surrounded by as many of the women as possible and have a full view of the rest.

Lisa and Rachel moved at a slower pace but were just as happy to be reunited with everyone once again.

"No Andrea tonight?" Lisa gave Ashley a knowing look.

Gemma shook her head. "I saw her in town on my way to meet Leo, but she said she has a meeting for the Historical Society tonight. It's been scheduled for weeks."

"Another day, then," Lisa said with an edge of disappointment, taking a chair at the end of the table. Rachel sat at the other head, already studying a drinks menu. With her hands on full display, Ashley couldn't help but notice that she wasn't wearing her wedding ring. She opened her mouth to question if Rachel had lost it but then decided it wasn't worth mentioning. No doubt her sister had forgotten to slip it back on after her shower. She'd certainly used up most of the hot water getting ready for this evening.

Ashley scanned the table. Already three glasses of sangria were in front of the first arrivals. "Why don't we order a pitcher?" She had nowhere to be, and she was used to staying up late.

Although, now that she thought about it, with all of her friends now paired off and married, she wasn't so sure how many more nights like this she would have.

"No one's driving," she joked. In response, Rachel gave a loud "har har" and then a little grin across the table. It was an old joke, one that never got old, especially on a carless island. Whenever they wanted to throw caution to the wind or go a little crazy, by ordering an extra dessert as kids, or, when their father came up for the weekends and had a nightcap, one of them would be sure to say it, pulling wan smiles all around.

Now, Ashley felt her smile slip, and, not wanting to let her good mood shift with the memories, she pushed her chair back. "Might be easier to order at the bar given the crowd. I'll get the first round!"

The room was air-conditioned, unlike the cottage, which relied on mother nature and ceiling fans, but Ashley felt a distinct burn rise in her cheeks when she spotted the man from yesterday sliding a glass of wine across the polished wood counter to a giggling group of women a few years younger than herself.

"Well, this is a surprise," she said, coming up beside the group and leaning into the bar top. He was even cuter than she remembered him, and she had remembered him, of course, even kept an eye out for him when she'd popped back into town, running errands for Lisa, who seemed to always need another item from the island's only hardware store.

The guy's dark eyes flashed with recognition and his grin broadened, revealing a rather adorable dimple.

"I was hoping I'd run into you," he said. "Was this fate or luck?"

Ashley felt the girl beside her bristle and then, with a huff, tell her posse to move back to a table. With an easy grin, Ashley slid into the vacant chair, deciding that her own group could wait a few extra minutes. Besides, they were probably so busy catching up, that they wouldn't even miss her. And she'd miss having to explain her life, her choices, her career. Or worse, talk about her mother.

"Neither," she said, batting her eyelashes. "It's a small island."

"Too small sometimes, but today, I can't complain."

"So, this is your bar." She looked around, taking in the nautical theme that wasn't too overdone, and, drawing from the crowd, one of the more popular establishments on the island. Some of the watering holes down near the docks could be rowdy, stuffed with tourists, but this crowd seemed more relaxed, and, noticing a few vaguely familiar faces as she scanned the room, local.

Ashley raised her eyebrows, impressed. "Why didn't I ever meet you before?"

"You tell me. I've been running this place for over five years now. How long has it been since you've been back?" he replied, popping the top on a beer and pouring its contents into a frosted glass.

"Too long," Ashley admitted on a sigh.

His brow quirked. "Too long indeed."

Biting her lip to hide her smile, she said, "I'm here with my sisters and our friends. Gemma Morgan?"

"I know Gemma," the man said. "But I don't know you."

Ashley laughed, realizing that they'd never been properly introduced. "Ashley Anderson."

He squinted at her. "The Andersons of the house up on West End Road? My, my, you're not just a local, you're a legend. That house is a part of this island's history."

Ashley swallowed uneasily when she thought of them handing it over to another family. "Yes, well, it's been a while. And you still haven't told me your name."

"Mack," he said, extending a hand.

She hesitated a moment before taking it, knowing that she was craving his touch more than she should. Sure enough, as his warm hand enveloped hers, holding it firmly, maybe a touch longer than one might consider simply friendly, she felt a ripple of tension in her stomach.

"Another round of sangrias?" he asked, starting the task.

"Thanks," Ashley said a little breathlessly. Before she could get too carried away, she walked back to the table, where everyone's eyes seemed to be on her every move.

"I can't believe you were talking with Mack!" Mandy said as soon as sat back down.

"Flirting is more like it," Rachel said, giving her a coy look that made Ashley roll her eyes. Leave it to Rachel to state the obvious.

"You and every other woman in town," Mandy lamented. "Well, except for me. That man will flirt with everyone in town, except for me."

Was this true? Normally, Ashley would have been amused by this, relieved even, to know that a guy wasn't looking for anything serious, that he was someone who liked a little fun and to keep it that way. But glancing back over her shoulder, to see him now serving another group of women a round of pink cocktails, she felt a prickle of something she couldn't quite identify. If she didn't know better, she might call it jealousy.

Well, that was just ridiculous.

"Mandy has been in love with him since the day he arrived on the island," Lena explained. "Running her family's sweet shop from just across the street hasn't exactly made it easier to forget about him, either."

"Hey, I'm plenty busy making ice cream!" Mandy protested, but her shoulders slumped a little when she glanced toward the bar.

Shoot. Ashley chewed her lip, thinking that she didn't want to upset her friend, even if they hadn't seen each other in over a decade.

"Well, you don't need to worry about me," she promised. "I'm not looking to start anything, and I'm only passing through."

"What's this I hear about passing through?" Ashley looked up to see Mack standing beside her, a grin on his face and a glimmer in his eye. He set the pitcher down. "You forgot this."

Ashley startled and glanced at the oversized pitcher. Had she? That wasn't like her. She was usually on top of things, organized, and careful when it came to keeping promises, which was why she never made one she didn't intend to keep.

"Must have been distracted," she said with a smile, ignoring the snort that she heard from somewhere across the table.

"Just gave me another chance to come over and see you again."

Ashley's heart began to race and she couldn't even imagine what Mandy was thinking now. Didn't even want to turn around and see her face.

She'd done nothing to invite this attention—well, not really. And she certainly wasn't giving off vibes of anything more than some fun on her vacation.

Which was probably why Mack was interested. Whereas Mandy had probably already started thinking about her wedding gown.

"Like I said. Small island."

His smile lingered a few minutes before he finally stepped away and, with a huge intake of breath, Ashley turned back to the table, bracing herself for the reaction.

Lisa was laughing, and Rachel was shaking her head. Gemma was trying to hide her own smile by biting down on her lip, and Lena was hiding her face behind her drink.

Ashley wasted no time in pouring herself one.

"I'm sorry, Mandy," she said, wishing that the night hadn't become awkward when it had started off so fun.

"No." Mandy shook her head quickly. "It's...just a crush. And an unrequited one at that. If Mack's going to set his eyes on someone other than me, I'd way rather it be you than one of these other girls that come in here night after night, drooling all over him."

"I was hardly drooling over him," Ashley said, taking a

sip of the sweet drink. Not only could the man make her heart flutter a little, but he also made a killer cocktail.

"Exactly," Gemma said. "And that's probably why he's still staring at you right now."

She glanced over Ashley's shoulder and then back to her, giving her a little wink that told Ashley that it would be okay. She hadn't upset their friend.

She'd just drawn the attention of the island's biggest playboy, known, it would seem, to break unsuspecting hearts.

But there would be no chance of him breaking hers.

13
LISA

Lisa stood at the kitchen counter, running water into a bucket and giving Ashley the stink eye. It wasn't fair, of course, especially when Ashley had volunteered to help clean out the carriage house, at least to dust off the bikes and maybe pump some tires. But there was Ashley now, sitting at the kitchen table near the back patio door, the one place in the house that seemed to have spotty cellular service.

And Lisa was itching to check her phone.

She wasn't expecting a message from Maisie. They'd had a brief call last night after Ashley had flirted with that cute bartender. She'd heard the phone ring and nearly leaped with excitement, and then of course immediately thought of a hundred things that could be wrong, because by then it would have been the middle of the night in France.

But Maisie was fine, just adjusting to the time, and she'd had the most wonderful evening, eating at a bistro, having dessert at a patisserie, and today she was going to be going with a group on a walking tour of the west bank.

It was everything that Lisa had once dreamed of doing, only she wasn't a part of any of it. Instead, she could only imagine Maisie taking in the sights and sounds and tastes and smells, exploring the city and describing it to her over a spotty connection.

She'd told herself that was okay, that she'd had her fun—well, sort of—and that she wouldn't want her daughter to miss out on this opportunity. And then, just before she'd come back into the pub, her phone had pinged again. That time it was Steve.

She hadn't read the long text or the other ones that followed it. Instead, she'd shoved the phone in her pocket, joined the girls, had some laughs and a few drinks, and told herself that see, this was the next phase of her life. Sort of. Because really, this was the last phase of her life being finally put to rest.

And Steve... She really shouldn't have tossed and turned half the night wondering what he had to say any more than she should be wishing her sister would stop sipping coffee and get off that chair, pronto.

She supposed she could go into town where service would be easier to find, but she had all the supplies she needed to finish the small projects that were within her wheelhouse. Going into town just to read her messages or reply to them or, worse, call back Steve was too much, even for her.

Even if she had considered it too many times to admit.

"I got a bucket of soapy water ready for you." Lisa gestured to the bucket, hoping it might encourage Ashley, but her younger sister just glanced up from her computer with a vague smile. "Sorry, are you working?"

"Drafting a post," Ashley confirmed. "I'll have to go into town, post it from a café later on."

Lisa stood a little straighter. "Oh, so, you'll be out in the carriage house for now?"

Ashley narrowed her gaze as she closed her laptop. "That eager to get your old bicycle out from all the dust and dirt?"

Lisa smiled easier. "It's the easiest mode of transportation around the island."

Ashley finished her coffee and finally stood, untangling her long legs from under her. "Okay, I'll go. But if you hear a blood-curdling scream, you'd better come running. You know I don't like spiders."

"And I do?" Lisa laughed, but it was true that in this old house, there were always spiders, and as the eldest of the lot, she was the one who had to toughen up and get the job done, while Ashley always fled from the room and Rachel claimed to be going after her to "make sure she was okay."

Not much had changed in all the years. Or enough, at least.

Ashley grunted as she took hold of the bucket. "Jeez. Did you need to fill it so full?"

"Careful not to slosh and slip!" Lisa called after her as Ashley inched her way to the door.

She stopped to give Lisa a scolding look over her shoulder. "Yes, Mom."

For a moment, the air felt sucked out of the room, because even though it was a joke, there was far too much truth in it for both of them. Ashley pushed through the door, her brow knitting, and hurried across the grass in her flip-flops, the water sloshing and making Lisa legitimately concerned she just might slip... But there she went worrying again.

And she had bigger things to worry about.

With a glance over her shoulder in case Rachel had decided to embark from her room for the day, she pulled her phone from her pocket and held it up in front of her, pacing the kitchen, searching for that magical bar, and for the unread messages to appear on her screen.

Her pulse leaped when the screen came to life and there, right in front of her, were three messages from her ex-husband. They varied in nature from asking about her trip, making sure she was safe, and of course, talking about Maisie.

A knock in the distance made her jump so hard she nearly dropped the phone in the wet sink. Scolding herself to get it together, she glanced at the clock, realizing that it was already nearly eleven and that it was probably the real estate agent she'd called before arriving here, scheduled to walk through the house and give her some feedback. She'd spent so much time alternating between trying not to think of Steve and wishing that Ashley would leave the kitchen so she could contact Steve, that the morning had slipped away, and now, well, now she had to answer the door.

It's for the best, she told herself, as she walked down the long hallway to the front door, opening it to greet the attractive woman on the other side.

"Lanie Thompson?" she asked, feeling a renewed surge of hope. Lanie looked to be in her early thirties, presentable in an A-line skirt and silk blouse, a far cry from the laid-back look of most islanders. She'd come by the ferry from Blue Harbor, where she was reported to be the top real estate agent in the county, at least according to Lisa's rather frenzied research.

"Lisa." Lanie gave a smile that was both warm, professional, and deeply reassuring.

Only now did Lisa realize just how badly she needed that. For someone to take away her troubles. To tell her that everything would be okay. That she didn't have to keep doing it alone, that they could share the burden. Because even though her sisters were both here in body, and Ashley was out back scrubbing out the carriage house or maybe just dodging cobwebs, neither of them understood the burden. And neither of them knew what it was like to worry about your child, or how each step you took could impact them.

That once she'd volunteered to take on the responsibility of this house to preserve it for her daughter, and now, she was hoping to sell it so that she could provide other things for her child.

None of this was about her. Even if a part of her heart would always live on in this house.

Lanie stepped inside, immediately noticing the scuffed floorboards that Lisa was yet to cover with one of the rugs she assumed was up in the attic, along with most of their other more expensive and personal effects. She kept her expression even as she lifted her chin, her eyes sweeping over the staircase, up to that ugly, sprawling, scary-looking water spot, and over toward the front living room.

"Well," she said, giving no true read into her thoughts,

though Lisa was sure she had some judgments. "Why don't you give me a tour and then we can discuss a strategy?"

A strategy. A plan. Yes, this was what Lisa needed! Normally she depended on Rachel for such things, but Rachel had been strangely uninterested in the fate of this house, or in the process of unloading it.

But then, this house carried a lot of emotion, for all of them, and Rachel had always been a master of keeping her emotions tied up in a neat bow.

Lisa started with the downstairs, showing Lanie through the sunlit living room to the darker, very unused, and oversized formal dining room, and then onto the kitchen, the library, and the sunroom, which, being at the back of the house, wasn't as appreciated as the front porch, at least when they came during the summers. Lanie took notes in a leather-bound folio, pausing to point out details of the architecture that Lisa was pleased to hear made the house special—or at least more valuable. When they came to the upstairs and the tour of the five bedrooms, with only a brief glance into Rachel's room, who was sitting at her childhood desk like a teenage girl and not a thirty-something woman, Lisa braced herself at the landing.

Lanie pointed a manicured finger at the offensive water stain on the ceiling. "I have a guy for you. He's from Blue Harbor, but he does a lot of work on Evening Island. I'll give you his contact information before I leave. There's more to fix there than just the ceiling."

Lisa felt her shoulders sink. "I know." Of course, she knew. And she knew about all the other hidden little problems that would show up in an inspection too. But what could people expect? This house was over a hundred years old!

"What do you think about the list price?" Lisa whispered once they'd reached the front hall again. It felt almost sacrilegious to be discussing the house like an object, like a product, something that she could give away, much less sell. She wanted to cover the photos of her grandparents that still rested on the mantle in the adjacent room.

"Let me look at some comps and get back to you on that," Lanie said. "It's tricky. A house this large, with this view, well, it doesn't come along very often. But it also requires a very unique buyer. It's not just about money. This is a remote island. Without cars. It's the ultimate place to get away and escape reality, but it's also not for everyone."

That gnawing cramp in Lisa's stomach had returned as Lanie spoke. Perhaps sensing her anxiety, Lanie suddenly flashed a big smile and said, "Before I forget. Let me write down the name of that contractor for you. Cole can probably stop by for a quote today if you call him soon."

She opened her portfolio and scribbled something down, then ripped the paper with a flourish.

Lisa took the paper back into the kitchen with the intent to call him straight away, the moment she got that bar of service, even though she wasn't so sure how much more bad news she could handle for one day. The project would be big. The quote could be enormous. And even though it wasn't coming out of her personal account, there was only so much money in the bank for this old place—and she knew that her parents wouldn't be contributing further. With their hearts, or their checkbooks.

She unlocked her phone with the simple code she would never forget (Maisie's birthday) and hovered over the messages button for a moment before shaking her head, silently scolding herself. She had a call to make but to Cole the contractor, not Steve the ex-husband who was officially dating someone else.

She dialed the number purposefully, but the reception faded before the connection was made, meaning a trip to town would be needed, after all, meaning that all the other little things on her to-do list would have to wait. And it was already Wednesday.

A muffled sound pulled her attention to the window over the sink. Ashley was calling out to her from the yard, waving her hands over her head, beckoning her.

Of course, Lisa thought, with a heavy sigh. Another problem to solve. She really was the mom now, and not just for her own daughter. Because her own daughter was in France and didn't need her at all.

"Yes?" She walked over to the back door, her voice was strained through the screen.

"Get your shoes and join me!" Ashley called with a devilish grin. "I have our bikes ready! Let's go for a ride!"

It was just like Ashley to suggest something fun when there was real work to do—something Rachel would have scoffed at, but then, Rachel wasn't here at the moment, was she?

A part of Lisa knew that she should refuse, go into town and run her errands instead, make her call—one only—and hurry back to work on the house. But her kid sister was inviting her to do something they hadn't done in over a dozen years. Something that she'd once taken for granted.

Something that, after they left this place, she could never do again.

Her sister might not know all the burdens worrying her mind, but somehow, she still knew just what she needed.

14
RACHEL

If Rachel had been sitting on the couch reserved for her troubled patients, questioning why she had watched her two sisters come around the side of the house, walking their old bicycles beside them, and then, when they had called up to her a moment later from the front hall, inviting her to join them, and why she had then run into the bathroom and ignored them, she knew the very thing she would have told herself.

And it was the very thing she did tell herself, as she sat on the edge of the clawfoot tub, under the skylight, staring up at the fluffy white clouds. She should get outside and get some fresh air. Put aside the book for a moment—she wouldn't be running away from it, just letting it rest. Taking some space. Clearing her head.

That sitting here, with just the silence, with only her own thoughts to keep her company, was not helping things at all.

With that decision made, ten minutes after her sisters had given up and left without her, she went downstairs, pushed out the back door, and began the march across the grass to the carriage house, where her old buttercup yellow cruiser was propped against the side of the building. It had been recently wiped down, left to dry in the sun, and when she checked the tires for pressure, it was clear that they'd been tended to as well.

Her heart warmed at the thought of one of her sisters making such a simple gesture on her behalf. That no matter how much she'd pushed them away, or kept them at a distance, they still cared.

They were still united. At least here. For now. By this house, and all the parts of it they'd shared.

Unlike the other old habits of this house, which seemed to come in waves, sneaking up on her when she least expected them to, riding the bike did not come as easily. The handlebars shook as she tried to get her footing, starting off slowly on the dirt road behind the house, wondering if she should call it quits by the time she'd circled around, through a sprint of woods that offered the best shade, and passed the front of the house. West End Road was downhill, and the angle only increased on the way into town.

It was reckless to be out here without a helmet! Of course, they'd never worn them as kids either. Half the time, Ashley hadn't even worn shoes, just pedaled all over the island from dawn until dusk with Ellie Morgan and Kimberly Taylor, stopping home for food or water, dropping into bed at night, exhausted and content.

By the time Rachel was past the big old hotel with its beautiful stallions and old-fashioned carriages standing proudly outside the grand entrance, she had found her groove, but that didn't stop her from applying the brakes down the worst of the big hill, remembering now how one of the Taylor girls had fallen one year, ended up in the Island Hospital, not that she was badly injured, but she certainly had a story to share. Rachel laughed out loud when she recalled how she and Heather Taylor and Gemma had decided to make it the front-page story in their neighborhood newspaper, which mostly focused on the details of the people who lived in those three Victorian homes at the base of West End Road.

A few tourists walking up to the hotel gave her a funny look as she laughed her way down the slope, the wind in her face and the speed of the bicycle making her feel like she was flying. Or losing it. Either way, for that one, fleeting moment, she felt better than she had in days. Maybe, even years.

As she approached town, the streets became more congested with tourists crossing with shopping bags, navigating rented cruiser-style bicycles with matching wire baskets to hold their belongings, and horses in shades of brown and grey. Slowing her pace, she scanned the crowds, knowing that it was no use trying to find Ashley or Lisa. They had at least a ten-minute advantage on her—more like twenty if she factored in her shaky start—and they could have gone anywhere by now. One of Lisa's favorite parts of the island to explore was Forest Bluff, up on the cliffs where the large homes were tucked behind towering walls of arborvitae, each one like a mystery, waiting to be discovered.

But that neighborhood was on the other side of the island, and there was no use turning around now. Instead, she would enjoy her own ride. And now that she was out, she had to admit that it beat sitting upstairs in that house that was in desperate need of an evening breeze, staring at a stack of papers that just made her palms sweat and her heart race.

She was heading down toward the harbor when she heard her name being called. Careful not to collide with a family of bikers maneuvering their rentals, she pulled to the side of the road and looked around for the source, certain that it hadn't been one of her sisters' voices.

"Rachel! Rachel Anderson!"

Rachel looked across the road to see none other than Andrea Taylor calling out to her, a huge smile on her face, her arm raised in the air with the kind of determination that made Rachel's heart swell, confirming what Lisa had said the other night. Andrea was still Andrea, from the auburn hair to the cool elegance of her appearance, to the focus and drive that the younger girls on the street had relied on, and, in Rachel's case, admired.

Andrea paused to let a horse and buggy cross in front of her before hopping off the curb and dashing across the street.

"I would have recognized you anywhere, even though I have had my eye out for you girls."

Unlike their friend Gemma, Andrea was reserved, like her. Still, she was the first to lean in for a hug, even if it was a little less tight and lingering than Gemma's had been.

"I was so sorry to miss drinks last night. Work stuff. I'm sure you understand. Gemma told me you're a therapist now. And writing a self-help book!" Andrea looked impressed, but Rachel's smile felt tight.

"And I heard that you decided to move here full-time." She shook her head in wonder. "Of all of us girls to end up here year-round, I can't say you were the one I'd have pegged for it."

"It's certainly different, but I've never been happier." Andrea's smile reached all the way up to her eyes. "And trust me, no one is more surprised than I am. But sometimes life throws you into something you didn't plan on."

She could say that again. Straightening her shoulders, Rachel said, "Are you busy now, or do you have time to catch up?"

"Why don't you come in and see the hotel? I've been helping John with it."

"John?" Rachel was already aware of the relationship that Andrea had formed, but the shy smile on her friend's face told her that she wouldn't mind elaborating a little.

"John Bowen. He bought the hotel about two years ago now. He's done wonders to it all while preserving the integrity of the architecture and the heart of the island."

She spoke with such pride about the man that Rachel was curious to meet him. "I'd love a glass of lemonade," she admitted, walking her bike alongside Andrea, who kept a brisk pace, usually reserved for the city. "Tell me they still make a pink lemonade here even though it's switched ownership."

"Of course!" Andrea grinned. "And the famous cinnamon rolls."

Rachel's stomach grumbled. "Some things never go out of style."

"And some traditions are meant to last."

Rachel pulled in a breath as they stopped before the front of the hotel, which was medium-sized compared to the bigger resorts, but intimate and charming in a way that was unique to this island. She parked her bike out front, thinking that she'd never dare do such a thing back in Chicago or even in the bucolic suburb where Lisa lived. But here, there were bikes parked all over the curbs, outside of shops, hotels, and restaurants, so many that one might think they'd get mixed up at best, taken accidentally, but they never did.

Inside the space was nearly exactly as she remembered it, but fresher, brighter, and newer.

"It's even more beautiful than I remembered it," she sighed when they came to the big dining room at the back, with the floor-to-ceiling windows looking out over the water.

"Let's go onto the deck and catch up," Andrea said. She waved Rachel through one of the French doors and spoke quietly to a waiter as Rachel selected one of the tables at the end of the long porch, admiring the pool and cheerful yellow- and white-striped table umbrellas below. The lake was behind it, big and wide, stretching as far as an ocean, it sometimes felt.

"Will John be joining us?" Rachel asked once Andrea had returned.

"I just asked but was told he's in meetings all day." Andrea shook her head. "Funny to think how that was my life not so long ago. Meetings, pressure, eating on the run. It was all about the next pitch, the next promotion. Of course, John walked away from all of that, too, but this project does consume him. Still, it's personal. More of a passion project."

A passion project. Once Rachel had thought that about her book, but now, every word of it felt false and misleading. Who was she to advise anyone on how to bond with their spouse and what to look for in a partner? She'd thought she'd found her match with Marty.

And she'd clearly been wrong.

"It must be a big transition, going from a corporate life to living here." Rachel only knew the island from the summer, when tourists kept the energy level relatively high, at least here in the center of town. But winters this far north were harsh, and for a couple of the coldest months, it wasn't easy to get on and off the island, meaning tourism slowed down to the point where many businesses closed for the season.

"I thought it would be a bigger one than it is, actually." Andrea smiled up at the waiter when he placed two pink lemonades before them. "I also did the honor of ordering," she said once he'd left.

Rachel admired the drink. "I don't think I've had a pink lemonade since...well, probably since the last time I was here."

"Isn't it interesting how the fact that it's pink makes it taste better somehow?" Andrea grinned. "Simple pleasures. That's what this island is all about."

"My only simple pleasure most weeks is a decent glass of Chardonnay at the restaurant down the block from my apartment."

"At least you managed to find some work-life balance," Andrea said. "You managed to juggle marriage with a demanding career."

Had she, though? She'd thought that's what they both wanted: long days, short weekends, definitely not enough vacations. There was always the talk of next year, but the next year came along, and with it came another booked calendar, charity events, social obligations, and work conferences that couldn't be missed.

Marty had never complained. And she hadn't either.

But she also hadn't been completely satisfied, something she'd kept to herself. Now, she wondered if Marty had also been hiding his reservations. Or maybe, his regrets.

"Finding the one person you can live with for your entire adult life isn't easy," Rachel said mildly. Certainly not as easy as she'd portrayed it to be in the opening chapters of her now very rough draft.

"Maybe not, but I wasn't even open to it. My career was my priority, maybe even my first love. It took coming here and meeting John and being back in that old, rambling house to remind myself why I ever went into architecture in the first place."

Rachel gave a wistful smile. "You always appreciated these old homes more than the rest of us."

Guilt gnawed at her when she considered what Andrea might have to say about their plans. Lisa had been wise in suggesting they keep things to themselves for a while, and discretion came easily to Rachel, especially when it involved details of her own life.

"I did, and here I have the best of both worlds. In the city, it was like I was never satisfied, never...present. It was always about what was on the calendar for next week, next quarter, and even next year. I got to a point where I had to ask myself what I would do in thirty years when my career was mostly behind me. When I didn't have a husband or children. Or even much of a relationship with my family, let alone friends outside of work."

Rachel's smile felt tight as she sipped her lemonade. "It's easy to get caught on the wheel. I'm guilty of it myself."

"Yes, but you have a husband."

One that she neglected. And who neglected her. It was just as Andrea had said: their careers were their first loves. Their marriage was something they fit in when they had a free moment. And as for making time for friends or family... Well.

"Anyway, you do have a job here on the island, and I probably shouldn't keep you from it too much longer. Even though we're on island time, I know you well enough to know you take your work seriously."

Andrea grinned. "You're right. You can take the girl out of the city and all that."

"People don't change. Not entirely." But they did change their minds, Rachel thought sadly. And they often grew apart. Rallying herself, she pulled in a breath. "You're still the same Andrea I remember you to be, and that's what's always so nice about coming back here. A whole schoolyear could pass, or now, what, more than a dozen years, and all us girls were always able to pick up right where we left off."

"The sign of a true friend," Andrea agreed, pushing back her chair. "You know that Gemma's throwing a dinner party this weekend, right?"

A dinner party that was starting to feel more like a farewell party. It was something that the Taylors used to do, at the end of each summer.

"And will John be joining us?" She grinned, relieved for a chance to turn the topic of conversation off herself.

"Of course!" Andrea gave a contented sigh. "I think you'll really love him."

"I'm sure I will." Rachel gave a little wave, but her heart felt heavy as she walked her bike down the brick-paved path toward the road a few minutes later. From everything that Andrea said, it sounded like she would like John, and very much.

But as for love... More and more, Rachel just wasn't sure she was capable of it.

15
ASHLEY

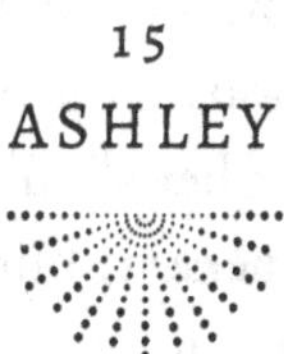

The front screen door banging shut roused Ashley from her slumber and she smiled as she rolled over to face the sunlight pouring through the part in the linen curtains. Another memory became clearer, one of her running into the house and back outside again, the screen door slamming behind her, her mother calling out to stop making so much noise.

That door—and the sound it made from her endless enthusiasm—were the sounds of summer. The sounds unique to that time in her life. To this house.

Pushing off the cotton quilt, she walked to the window, which didn't have a view of the lake, but rather faced the backyard with its overflowing perennial beds which had admittedly been neglected in recent years. It wasn't much used. The Taylors were the ones with the playhouse; the Morgans had a hammock. But all the Anderson girls craved was the front porch and that water that stretched out far before them.

Downstairs in the kitchen, Lisa was already hunched over

the counter, a cup of coffee warming her two hands that clutched the mug as if it were something she wouldn't part with easily.

"I'm afraid we're all out of coffee," she said when Ashley opened the cabinet that housed the mugs.

"Already?" Ashley felt her shoulders deflate. She considered herself a morning person, but a warm cup of coffee always got the day started a little easier. "Did Rachel go into town to get some?" she asked hopefully.

"She went for a run. You know how she loves to run."

Ashley was ashamed to realize that she didn't know that. She knew her middle sister was regimented, and more disciplined than she'd ever care to be, but as for Rachel's daily routine, Ashley supposed that it was as foreign a concept to her as her own preferences might be to her sisters.

Lisa, looking repentant, held out her mug. "You're welcome to a sip."

Ashley had to laugh at the thought of that. "Thanks, but I think I'll head into town and park myself at the café for a bit. Get some work in. If I don't post fresh content every few days, my sponsors get twitchy." She hesitated for a moment before leaving the room. "That is unless you need me around here all day?"

"No, go. You have other things to worry about in life than this old house," Lisa said in that motherly, caring way that Ashley had always depended on from her.

But Lisa wasn't her mother. She was her sister. And Ashley was no longer a child in search of someone to take care of her.

"And don't you? Have other things to worry about than this old house, I mean?"

Lisa seemed to hesitate for a minute and then smiled brightly. "With Maisie away for a few weeks, not really. This house has my full attention. Besides, it keeps me busy, and... it's sort of nice being back here."

Ashley nodded slowly. "It is," she said, and then left the room before she could dwell on it further. It *was* nice being back here. It was an escape like it had always been. And like always, the real world was a lot more confusing and much less reliable.

Wasting no time in changing into a cotton sundress and braiding her long hair, Ashley set her laptop in the basket of her bicycle and pedaled into town, parking her cruiser in front of the Cottage Coffeehouse.

As always, the rickety screen door was the only obstruction between the inside and outside, and already the outdoor tables were consumed by locals or summer people crouched over the island's newspaper, scones resting on plates forgotten for a moment.

Tourists didn't bother with this place as much as the bigger establishments on Main Street, and not because it wasn't wonderful. There were some places in town that were just for the locals. Where she was bound to run into her summer family, as she'd once called them.

Lena was standing behind the counter, wearing a crisp apron, her cheeks a bright pink as she foamed milk for the man at the cashier. Ashley smiled at her and used the time to study the sweets in the display case, thinking that since she didn't have to worry about fitting into a bridesmaid dress again any time soon, she had no reason not to indulge to her heart's content.

Finally, Lena handed the man his latte and turned her attention to Ashley. "I was hoping you'd come by to see me one of these days."

"I'm just sorry it's taken so long," Ashley said. "I've been helping Lisa fix up the house. You know how it is."

Of course. Anyone who owned property on the island did. These homes weren't new, and maintenance was made extra difficult by the remote location and lack of ease with transportation of supplies.

"These homes are a labor of love," Lena said fondly.

Ashley chewed her lip, thinking that usually, that would be the case, but not now. Lisa was eager to get the place restored, not because she cared about it anymore, but because she wanted it gone. She wanted to unload the responsibility, and could Ashley really blame her?

It wasn't like she was in a position to take it over herself... And would she even want to?

She blinked, shaking these crazy thoughts away. That's what a morning without caffeine did to her, all right. Made her mind go down strange paths.

"Coffee, please. Strongest and largest you have," she said.

Lena grinned. "Paper cup or a mug?"

"A mug. I'm camping out a bit," Ashley replied.

"Good, because I didn't get to spend nearly enough time with you the other night."

At the mention of their girls' night at Hackney's, Ashley felt her stomach stir. "I hope that wasn't weird...with Mandy." Ashley glanced over her shoulder to make sure that there wasn't a line forming behind her, but for now, it was clear.

"Don't worry about it. Mandy gets a little ruffled every time she sees Mack flirting with a girl, which is pretty often." Lena shook her head and began transferring a tray of cookies to a basket. "You'd think she'd be used to it by now."

"That bad, huh?" Ashley kept her eyes on the baked goods but her mind was trailing. Mack was a flirt, a regular one, too, from the sounds of it, meaning she was just another page in his playbook. She shouldn't be flattered; she should be turned off, or at the least, she should be pleased, to be off the hook, to know that he wasn't looking for more than she was willing to offer.

But for some reason, she felt oddly disappointed.

"It's probably because of the lack of options," Lena said with a shrug. She held out the basket, raising an eyebrow, but Ashley shook her head. With a sigh, Lena set the basket on top of the display case and said, "The island can be pretty quiet at times. Sometimes too quiet. You only remember the summer months."

Ashely didn't say anything. It would be a lie to agree because she had chosen not to remember anything. But it was all still there, tucked away, a part of her that she couldn't deny.

"When another handsome face comes along she'll be fine. And I think she knows that nothing will ever happen with Mack."

"He isn't looking for the same thing as her." Ashley nodded.

"Maybe." Lena looked thoughtful. "Or maybe there's

more to it. But the way I see it, if it was going to happen, it would have happened by now. One thing about Mack is certain."

Ashley realized that she was holding her breath. "What's that?"

"Mack isn't shy when he likes someone."

The expression told Ashley that Lena was talking about more than Mack right now. Her cheeks flushed and she was relieved to see another woman push through the rickety screen door, struggling with her shopping bags.

"I'll have one of those blueberry scones," Ashley said, and then, because she expected to be here for a while and she was all too happy to support Lena's business, she added, "And one of those brownies."

Lena grinned. "I already had one plated for you. There are some things in life you just can't resist. And shouldn't!"

No, but there were some things that you should.

Ashley took her coffee and plate and scanned the room, looking for a place to set up her laptop and maybe people-watch for a bit, but without too much distraction. When a young couple rose from a table in the corner near the front window, she hurried her pace across the room, feeling like she'd won a prize when she dropped into the chair triumphantly.

"You're not from around here, are you?" a man with hair that was greying at the temples watched her sternly over the top of the local newspaper.

Ashley opened her mouth and then closed it again. There was no point in mentioning that she'd spent every summer here until her mid-teens without inviting a conversation she didn't have the energy for. Besides, he was looking at her like she'd done something wrong, assuming that she was an outsider, that somehow, she didn't fit in.

"New York," she said, which wasn't exactly true either, considering she'd only lived there for a handful of years and hadn't committed to making it her permanent home. Nothing was permanent, and it was better to treat it as such.

"Ah." The man gave a little smirk and a nod.

Ashley bristled but said nothing more. She might live in New York but her heart... Well, never mind that.

Wasting no time, she opened her laptop and tapped in her password. Her screensaver sprang to life before her—one of all her "sisters" as she'd always called them, at a wedding last year. They were all lined up in lavender chiffon, only the bride in white. They were laughing, smiling, their arms wrapped around each other. For a long time, seeing this photo every day made her feel completely content. Reminded her that she'd pulled through, and found her people.

But being here with her actual sisters this past week overshadowed that warm and comforting feeling, reminding her that as close as she was to her friends, her real sisters were the ones who shared her history. And her childhood.

Ashley pulled open a fresh post page and began writing. And then stopped. She'd already written extensively about the most recent wedding, and with none on the horizon, she was in danger of running out of fresh material. She thought about what her sisters had suggested. She could shift the blog in a new direction by adding more content and broadening its readership, but diversifying could also mean diluting her brand, and right now, it was a one-stop shop for wedding inspiration, from gowns to flowers, to the little details like bridesmaid gifts (she had an entire drawer of them ranging from pretty necklaces to makeup bags with broken zippers).

She'd be the first to admit it: she liked the blog as it was. And now that was a problem. Its time was running out along with her ideas. Without another wedding on the horizon, what was there to even write about?

She'd gone and done the one thing she'd promised herself to never do. Get comfortable. With a house, with a man. And it would seem now, with a career.

"Is this seat taken?"

She looked up to see Mack, standing beside the table, grinning at her. Her cheeks flamed and she darted her gaze to the counter, where Lena was giving her a knowing look that she was grateful Mack wouldn't see unless he turned around.

Unfortunately, Mack's attention had drifted to the photos on her screen, along with the headline, which was rounding up the best cakes from the last six weddings she'd attended.

Just thinking of that scoring system made her think of Michael. Another reason why it was good to know that Mack, much like herself, had absolutely no interest in anything other than fun.

"You planning a wedding?"

"Me?" Ashley laughed, loudly. The grumpy man next to her lowered his paper and gave her a stern look, but she ignored him. "God, no. No wedding plans for me." Ever, she finished to herself.

"Good." Mack grinned broadly and dropped into the chair.

Ashley closed her laptop, unsure if he meant good that she wasn't interested in marriage or that she wasn't involved with someone.

Oh, what did it matter? That was the beauty of casual relationships or even flings. There was no need to analyze. No need to worry about who should make the next move or if it was too early to call, or if he would call. There were no expectations and no promises, either. There was just the here and now. What happened tomorrow was of no concern or consequence.

"This is my job, actually," she said. "I write a blog. About weddings."

"Please don't tell me you're one of those girls with a huge binder full of clippings and a reservation at the country club five years out," Mack said, but he delivered it with a smile.

"Um, no. I'm the girl who has eighteen bridesmaid dresses in my closet," she replied. Before he could ask, she raised a hand. "Sorority sister."

"A popular one, too." He looked amused as he sipped his coffee. "And an opportunistic one."

Ashley laughed. "Maybe. Or just savvy. But when you attend that many weddings and hear about each one for months on end, and know every single detail, well, you start to live it, too."

"Living vicariously, then?"

"Exactly." Ashley nodded firmly. "I'm...ready for a break from weddings for a while." And that was just the problem, she thought, glancing back at the laptop.

"And that's the reason you're here?"

"Partly," she said because she didn't exactly feel like elaborating on the house. Besides, she wasn't looking to get deep with this man. She was looking for fun. And something in the intensity of his deep-set gaze told her that he was too.

"And you haven't told me how long you're in town for," he said, lifting an eyebrow.

Now Ashley answered honestly. "Because I don't know the answer myself. I'm sort of taking things day by day."

"And might there be a day in there for me?"

Oh, he was bold. And she didn't mind.

She gave a little mew, but she struggled to hide her smile completely. "What did you have in mind?"

"I have tomorrow afternoon off," he said, giving her a slow grin.

"Tomorrow probably works," she said.

"It's a date then," he said, standing up.

Ashley pursed her lips, wondering if she should correct him, but then decided to let it slide. What did it matter what he called it? That was the beauty of keeping things cool. Call it what you want, it didn't matter, because, at the end of the day, they'd both go their separate ways, and be totally fine with that.

16
LISA

Lisa was outside, weeding the garden, when the phone rang. She startled, dropping the handful of dandelions she'd pulled from the flower bed. The sound was still so unfamiliar, almost intrusive, cutting through the silence that was otherwise the backdrop here on the island, only the sounds of nature, or the occasional rickety sound of a bicycle breaking up the quiet.

Pulling off the muddy gloves she'd found in the carriage house, she took the phone from her back pocket, hoping that it was Maisie and worried that she would miss her.

But it wasn't Maisie. It was Steve.

Normally, she'd always take Steve's calls. Looked forward to them, even. Their chats were daily, sometimes even more than once a day, usually about Maisie, often segueing into other topics. The conversations had started only because they'd never stopped. Just because Steve had moved out didn't mean that their interaction had ceased—if anything it became less stressed, less forced, less full of all the resentment that had built up over those early years when they'd struggled to grow into their responsibilities. Now there was an ease she shared with him that she'd never found with anyone else—not even her sisters. There was no pretense, no thinking of what to say next. It was natural. Comfortable. Like a favorite sweater on the first chilly day of autumn.

Only now, she did have to think about what to say. Because now all she could think about was that for as much as they talked, and shared, there was something that Steve had withheld from her.

The phone rang once more, and despite herself, she answered it. He was her child's father, after all. It wouldn't be responsible for her to let it go.

Besides, maybe he had news on Maisie. Maybe, she thought, her heart beginning to pound so hard that for a moment she felt shaky, something had happened to Maisie. Maybe Maisie had tried to call her when she didn't have reception. Maybe the call had gone straight to voicemail and Lisa was none the wiser.

But Steve's voice was its usual blend of warm and jovial when he said, "You're alive!"

"I was worried that something had happened to Maisie," she said, still needing to be sure.

"I spoke to her last night. She said she already talked to you twice since you've been on the island." There was a beat that told Lisa that Steve wasn't finished with that thought. "Here I thought you had no service or something."

Darn it, his tone sounded a little injured, and what right did he have to feel that way? They were divorced—had been for years! And he was seeing someone else.

She didn't need to be in daily contact, especially not when Maisie wasn't around as the excuse.

But now she wondered, as she idly walked the perimeter of the lawn, stopping to pull another cluster of dandelions, if this was about Maisie at all.

"I saw your texts." She paused, wondering what to say, and feeling sad that she even had to think about it. She'd never had to watch herself until now, never had to worry. Steve was reliable, the person she trusted most in this world. The person who knew her best too. There was no need for pretense or games. But now she felt the need to hold back. To protect herself.

To protect her heart, she realized, as her stomach twisted with unease.

"I wasn't able to reply. As you can imagine, there isn't much service around here. We might get cut off," she warned.

She wasn't sure if she wished it would happen or not.

"How was your call with Maisie?" she needed to know.

"Fine, brief. Made me realize that she's growing up." Steve's tone matched her own emotions. It was all too easy to picture Maisie as a little girl with bangs and chocolate around her mouth than a young woman alone in a foreign country, preferring the company of her friends to her parents.

"Time flies," Lisa said, looking up at the old house that rose above her into the cloudless blue sky. It felt like she blinked and she was already in her mid-thirties, all the things she'd hoped for in life chosen or decided upon by now, when she'd still been dreaming about them the last time she was here.

She shielded her eyes against the blinding sun. It was a warm day, and there weren't any trees to lend any shade in the yard. Deciding to risk losing the connection, she climbed the back steps to the kitchen door in search of a cold glass of water.

"Makes me even more determined to make the most of the rest of the time we have with her," Steve said.

Now, as she filled a glass, Lisa had to laugh. "She's only fifteen, and I hate to break it to you, but the next few years will be long ones. I've had enough experience with teenage sisters to tell you that there will be a day where you can't wait for her to be all grown up."

"Maybe." Steve sighed. "How are your sisters? Maisie mentioned that Ashley was there?"

Lisa swallowed back the water. The connection was breaking up, so she scooted closer to the door. "Yup. That was certainly a surprise, but...a good one. It's been nice, all being here at the house again. It's like nothing has changed. The Taylors are here, and the Morgans too. At least most of them. It's weird to think that everything has continued just as it was even when I wasn't here to enjoy it."

"Funny how that works, isn't it?"

Lisa frowned, unsure what Steve meant by that, when she heard a knock in the distance. Startled, she set down the water glass and glanced at the old clock that hung beside the refrigerator.

The contractor! The last piece in getting this house fixed up and the most important one, too.

She hurried down the hall and waved through the glass before turning the locks and letting the man inside.

"You don't know how happy I am to see you," she told him.

"Happy to be here," the man replied with a broad, setting down his toolbox.

"Who's that?" Steve's tone sounded troubled.

"Look, can we talk later?" Lisa motioned to the contractor that she was wrapping things up.

"I was thinking..."

Lisa squinted and pulled the phone from her cheek. She was somehow still connected, but she was losing the call quickly.

"We have a bad connection. I can't hear you," she said loudly, walking quickly to the back of the house, to the corner of the kitchen where she might have better luck.

"I was saying that when you get back should go to dinner so you can tell me all about your trip."

"I'll probably be here for another week at least. Maisie's still going to be in France then," she reminded him. She couldn't deny the pang in her chest when she said those words out loud. Maisie. In France. Without her.

"I know, but that doesn't mean we can't spend time together, does it?"

Lisa froze. Technically, it did. Or it should. Because they were divorced. They'd chosen to end their marriage years ago, and it had been the right thing to do, for all of them. The arguments had stopped when the resentment faded, and they'd been able to come together and still give Maisie all the love and time and affection that they both wanted for her.

It was the best of both worlds, or so she told herself when things felt a little muddled and old habits crept in.

But maybe it was more than that.

Or maybe, she thought, thinking of Steve's romantic dinner date, it wasn't.

Maybe, Steve had news to share. An announcement to make.

"I should go. I have someone waiting for me," she said hurriedly against the pounding of her heart.

"I wouldn't want to keep you," Steve said, before disconnecting the call.

If she didn't know better, she'd say that Steve sounded jealous. But she did know better, because she knew now that Steve had let go of her long before she'd let go of him. Or, rather, them.

* * *

Lisa watched as the contractor stood high on the ladder and, with one fell swoop, punched a hole in the offensive water mark, releasing a shower of water that fell mostly into the buckets he'd set up, and what didn't onto the faded and threadbare towels that had once been a bright blue and were now more of a pale grey.

Anxiety roiled her stomach, but he didn't seem deterred. Deciding that this was progress and not a setback and that hovering would do neither of them any good, she grabbed a broom from the closet and went out onto the porch, determined to make herself busy. And keep herself busy.

She would not pull her phone from her pocket and attempt to find service. She would sweep this entire porch free of cobwebs and dirt and then she'd retouch the paint where needed.

How was that for a distraction?

She lasted all of four minutes before her mind began to wander again. What did Steve mean, wanting to have dinner? Was he—she felt herself pale on the sudden thought—getting married again?

It was possible. But somewhere over time, she had stopped thinking that it was. Not just for her, but for both of them.

She stood up, to check her phone once and for all, when she saw a familiar face coming down the road. All thoughts of Steve were forgotten as she held up a hand and called out.

"Andrea Taylor!" It didn't matter that she knew Andrea was on the island. Seeing her, after all this time, came as a surprise. And an emotional one, she realized, feeling a warmth spread over her entire body as she dropped the broom and darted down the porch stairs to greet her old friend.

A big hug and a moment later, they made their way up the steps, all thoughts of using the afternoon to improve the house forgotten.

"Can I get you a lemonade?"

"I'm fine," Andrea assured her as she moved to take a wicker chair. "Just your company is more than enough. Now sit. Tell me everything."

"I don't even know where to begin!" Lisa looked back on the sixteen years since they'd been in touch and realized just how much had happened in her life...and maybe, how little she had to show for it. "Where did things leave off that last summer?"

"You were dating a guy in college that you really liked," Andrea said.

"Steve. Well, shortly after I got pregnant with Maisie. She's fifteen now, if you can believe it."

"Is she here?" Andrea looked hopefully toward the door.

"No, she's away for the summer. And Steve and I divorced several years ago."

"I'm sorry to hear that," Andrea said, sounding like she meant it.

"It's okay," Lisa said lightly. "We've made it work." At least they had, until now.

"Anyone special in your life?" Andrea waggled her eyebrows.

For a moment, Lisa almost said that of course there was someone special. There was Steve. But of course, Andrea meant a new boyfriend, or more.

She shook her head, feeling her heart speed up in anticipation of having to defend her single status as she did with Rachel. "My daughter keeps me busy enough."

"I can imagine! Not that I have kids myself. It's all work for me. Or at least, it was...until I moved here last summer."

"Ah, yes, but you must still be busy with work if it kept from coming out with us all for drinks the other night."

Andrea laughed. "Guilty as charged. I've told myself I have to stop focusing on work, especially since moving here, but as they say, you can take the girl out of the city..."

"Or off the island," Lisa added, thinking how true it was.

No matter where she was, a part of her was still linked to her past. Try as she might to move on from it.

"What about you? Somehow I always pictured you being some sort of interior designer. You always had a way of making a house a home, whereas I was more about the house itself." Andrea shook her head. "I'm just glad to be away from that soul-sucking architecture firm and back here, where I got my inspiration."

"And found love?" Lisa smiled.

Andrea's smile was coy. "It finds you when you least expect it."

Or leaves you when you least expect it, Lisa thought sadly. Because somehow, the thought of Steve moving on now cut deeper than it had when they'd first split up.

"Well, work is all I have other than Maisie, and you're close. I run a gift shop, but not one with postcards or picture frames. I like to pull unique items from all over the world and keep everything feeling fresh. And special."

"You haven't changed one bit, Lisa Anderson," Andrea said with a knowing smile.

Lisa sighed wistfully. If only that were true. Because right about now, she'd do anything to go back to that last summer here on the island, when she was only nineteen years old, and do it all differently.

But there was one thing she wouldn't change. Maisie was the one part of her life that she'd gotten right.

17
RACHEL

The noise in the hallway was a welcome excuse for Rachel to step away from the draft of her book which she was now tempted to delete. And she'd intended to do just that following her morning run—told herself that she would start from scratch, because everything she'd written, and everything she'd claimed to be true, was a lie.

Including her own marriage.

But a hot shower had calmed her down and she'd instead spent the day reviewing what she'd written, laughing almost bitterly at how sure of herself she'd sounded in the opening pages. How...smug. As if she held the magic formula for a long and happy marriage.

She'd gotten comfortable in her relationship with Marty. Viewed it as something as black and white as the paper she'd written on. Thought that she'd found a sure thing rather than fall down the disastrous path her mother had. She'd led with her head, not her heart.

Somedays, she wasn't even sure she had a heart. Now, she

wondered if that was the problem. If something was missing. Something that she could live without but maybe Marty couldn't.

Something like a child.

She'd told herself over the years that she was fine with their choice, and decided not to voice her doubts to Marty, even when, as the years passed, they seemed to deepen. Now, she wondered if Marty had had doubts too.

Or if his doubts were about her.

She opened the bedroom door to see a man in jeans and a navy tee shirt standing on a ladder on the landing, poking at a giant hole in the ceiling. Buckets and thoroughly soaked towels covered the floorboards, and he glanced down at her with a grin that bordered on apologetic.

"Sorry. I didn't realize anyone else was here. You weren't napping, were you?"

For the first time in days—if not longer—Rachel let out a laugh. "Napping? No. No, I do not nap."

Napping was for people like her sister Ashley. People who had time to fritter away. People who weren't worried about tomorrow and certainly not planning for it.

People who had free time. And Rachel never had free time. She'd made sure of that. Even here, the one place where that was all she once had. Long days, longer evenings, weeks that seemed to drag on forever with no end, not that she was looking forward back then.

No, back then she lived the moment. All the planning, all the goal-setting, that had come later, until it became all she had.

The man was giving her a quizzical look now, and he'd

come down a few rungs on the ladder to give her a proper introduction.

"Cole the contractor, right?" Rachel prided herself on remembering the passing comment from Lisa when the real estate agent first handed over the contact information. Her listening skills were what made her a great therapist, but the advice she gave was still in question.

Extending his hand, he said, "I'm Ray. I work with Cole."

"Rachel," she said, giving a shy smile when she realized that their names had a similar sound. For some reason it made her feel bonded to him, more than the strong, confident hand that shook hers, more than that lingering grin that crinkled around his very blue eyes.

She snatched her hand back, swallowing hard. "I was just...working."

"Oh." Now Ray cringed, looking guilty. "Lisa didn't mention it. I'll try to keep it down."

"No problem," Rachel said lightly. "I was just about to take a break anyway." And she couldn't really constitute worrying and procrastinating as work anyway, could she?

Suddenly aware that this was awkward, and that she didn't want to give the impression that she was looking for someone to talk to or keep her company, even though that was actually exactly what she was doing, she said, "I was just about to go downstairs. To see my sisters."

"Ah, I thought I saw the resemblance to Lisa." He grinned as he moved back up the ladder with ease. "It's the smile."

The man had noticed her smile. She grinned a little

broader and felt a heat flush up her cheeks. Her eyes seemed to blink rapidly, nearly batting his way! What was she doing? The man was here to work, to fix that giant, molding hole in the ceiling, and she... Well, she was going to look for her sisters, have a glass of iced tea, and then get back to work.

"Lisa's the oldest," she said because she wasn't a fan of awkward silence. "Not that she's old, but I mean, she's probably, oh, about your age."

And she had officially spent too much time on this remote island. She'd tucked herself away for too long, inside that old bedroom. Yes, that was it. Cabin fever. There was a diagnosis for everything if you thought about it long enough.

Ray gave her another quizzical look as he worked at the hole, and Rachel, eager to get downstairs, carefully moved around the debris and towels and then slinked down the stairs quickly, relieved once she was in the hallway, which she all but dashed through to get to the kitchen.

A few minutes later, while she was boiling tea to then cool and ice, she heard Lisa's voice on the stairs, talking to Ray. His tone was deep but light, and although she couldn't make out the words of the exchange, there was a sudden burst of laughter, before a scraping of metal sounded, and a moment later, heavy boots on the stairs.

"I'll see you tomorrow then?" Lisa's voice sounded lighter than it had in days, not that Rachel was eavesdropping. She was simply waiting for her tea to steep, and she was trained to pay attention to these things, to listen, to understand.

"See you then. Bye, Lisa," Ray said, and then, almost

making Rachel slosh the hot beverage, he called out, "Bye, Rachel!"

"Bye!" she said, poking her head into the hallway. Her heart beat a little faster when she caught his grin before he pulled the door closed behind him.

Ridiculous! Absolutely ridiculous to be so thrilled by male energy in this house—another symptom of being cut off from civilization.

"Well," she said, once Lisa had come back to the kitchen. "He was certainly handsome." She gave her sister a pointed look.

"Was he?" Lisa opened the fridge and studied the contents, then closed it again. "I didn't notice."

Rachel continued to stare at her, wondering if her sister could be this oblivious or, worse, this in love with her ex-husband. Rachel liked Steve; he was a friendly guy and a great father, she knew. More of a sporty type than Marty, which had never leant itself to couples' dinners, but then, Maisie had been in the picture long before Rachel and Marty had met, and of course, their social circle was adults only.

And of course, now Lisa and Steve were divorced. It hadn't come as a surprise, not really. They'd married young, under pressure, and struggled financially with a young baby. While other kids their age were finishing up college, Steve was getting work at his father's insurance company, something he resented. There were arguments. Lots of them. There were fears. Probably more than Lisa ever voiced to her. The deck was stacked against them. Nothing in Rachel's professional opinion would have made them a contender for the long haul.

And yet… And yet when Lisa told her that Steve had moved out, Rachel had been silently crushed. She'd never said it to Lisa, of course, but a part of her had dared to hope that maybe Lisa could break the curse and rewrite history. Prove her wrong.

"You didn't catch that grin?" Rachel certainly hadn't missed it, not any more than those bright blue eyes, either. "He was smiling at you."

"Oh, stop it!" But Lisa was blushing now, looking positively girlish and flustered as she tidied the already clean kitchen. "Guys don't notice me."

"Why shouldn't they?" Rachel felt annoyed at the way her sister always put herself in a box, refusing to open a window, much less her mind to anything new.

"I don't know. Because I'm…thirty-five."

"You're only two and a half years older than me," Rachel countered.

"Because I'm divorced."

Rachel almost laughed. Did her sister forget what line of profession she was in? But then she considered that soon, she might also be part of that club, and felt a twinge of sorrow. "Lots of people are divorced, Lisa."

Their parents, she knew, were at the forefront of their minds. Being back in this house made it impossible not to think of that last summer here, and all the summers before it, and how different it all was when it ended.

"Well, then, because I have a teenager," Lisa insisted, picking up a dish rag and then tossing it back in the sink. She moved on to the tea towels, embroidered with patterns of lilacs, a flower that the island was famous for, making it a common theme in the local shops that their mother once frequented.

"You can't tell that by looking at you. Besides, what does that change?"

Now Lisa turned around and gave her a hard look. "A lot. Having a kid changes a lot. It means that everything I do, say, and choose is with her in mind. It means that I'm not thinking about myself much anymore, even though I know you think I should. It's not that easy, in fact, it would be selfish. She's my responsibility. She's my priority."

Rachel wasn't used to this kind of outburst from her sister and wasn't exactly sure where it was coming from, or if she wanted to know. "Whoa. I was just saying that a good-looking guy was being friendly with you, that's all."

"I know what you really think," Lisa said, shaking her head. "You don't understand a lot of my choices. Why I'm a homebody. Why I still spend so much time with Steve."

Ah, now they were getting somewhere.

"Maisie matters most to me. When she was born, heck, even before she was born, everything I did was with her well-being in mind. And that's just something that you wouldn't understand, even with all of your fancy degrees."

Rachel felt as if she'd been slapped. She knew objectively that her sister was talking about herself, being defensive, but there was an undertone of judgment there that she couldn't help take personally because it tapped into the one part of her that she had now started to question.

Was she selfish? And what would life be like if she did decide to have a child?

Would she be any good at it? Or would she fail, and

would she end up making the same mistakes that her own parents had?

She plucked an apple from the bowl on the counter and moved back into the hallway, deciding that there was no use in pondering that thought unless she wanted to torture herself. She'd made her decisions. Honored them even if she didn't always truly want to accept them.

And where had that gotten her? Alone, in this house, with one sister who was nowhere to be found most of the time, not that this was particularly surprising, and another who may as well have stayed back in her little house on the north side of the city, making her entire life about two other people who had both left her in some way or another.

Rachel could never put herself in that position. She'd made the choice not to. Instead, she had her career. Her book. And even if she might not be an expert in marriage, after all, she was at least an expert in not setting herself up for further hurt.

With that, she hurried up the steps, determined to get a few more pages done in her book. Knowing that it was at least one thing she still had. If she didn't go and mess that up too.

18
ASHLEY

Mack was waiting for her outside the Cottage Coffeehouse as they'd agreed upon—and Ashley was happy to see that she wasn't the first to arrive. She wasn't late, either, which made her wonder just how long he'd been sitting at the bistro table, sipping a coffee.

Her heart swooped as he stood up and greeted her with a kiss on the cheek.

Steady there, she warned herself. It was just a peck on the cheek. Appropriate, because a handshake would have been too stiff and there was no denying what was happening here. They were on a date. A casual one, but a date nonetheless.

And she was no stranger to dates. So why then was she suddenly a little nervous in his company?

Mandy, she told herself. Lena was no doubt inside the café right now, seeing the two of them together again. Word would spread to Mandy, and the last thing Ashley wanted to do was hurt her feelings.

But then, Mandy had given up on Mack. She'd said so.

Lena had said so. And that was a very poor excuse for how Ashley felt right now as Mack tossed his paper cup into the bin and said, "Shall we?"

He offered her the crook of his elbow and she slipped her arm through companionably as they walked down the sidewalk, past small clapboard buildings that housed artwork from the island's many painters.

Ashley kept an eye out for another piece from Ellie, but nothing struck her, and at the moment, she was a little distracted.

"Where are we going?"

"Well, I'd offer to show you all the best parts of the island, but I have a feeling that you could probably do a better job of that," he said, giving her a sideways look. "But it's warm. I thought maybe we could grab some sandwiches at the bakery, take them over to a part of the waterfront that the tourists don't know about?"

"Sounds good to me," she said, and she realized that she'd come along today with no expectations. It wouldn't have mattered if he'd offered to ride horses or bikes or even if he'd said they were taking the ferry over to the mainland for the day. She'd agreed to come along simply for the pleasure of his company.

Careful. The little voice warned her as they walked down to Main Street and soon came upon the Island Bakery. They picked up two sandwiches on crusty, freshly made baguette, promising to share, two fizzy drinks, and of course, two slices of pie, which Mack admitted he might not be willing to share, which of course made her smile.

He was charming, and far too easy on the eye, and it was

no wonder why every single woman on the island had a spot in their heart for him, and why every tourist had their sights on him instead of the open water, the lush greenery, and the charming houses that usually drew people to Evening Island.

They took their time heading out of town in the direction opposite her home—past the church, and the building that was once Ellie's studio and was now Leo's law office. Past the harbor, and the Lakeside Inn, which Rachel said Andrea's boyfriend now owned and that yes, they did still have cinnamon rolls and pink lemonade, even if the two were never consumed together.

At the water's edge where the road curved north was another large inn and a park where people sat on picnic baskets, enjoying the panoramic view of the water. It was a popular spot, and Ashley was secretly pleased when Mack showed no signs of stopping. He knew the island as well as she did—even if she hadn't thought about it in years. Up ahead she knew that people might pass by on bikes, but few would stop along the rocky shoreline. And there was where they settled.

"This is one of my favorite spots on the island," Mack said, settling onto one of the boulders that was large enough for them to both fit.

"Really? Mine too."

"But you're directly across from the water over on West End Road," he said, giving her a funny look.

"Yes, but I liked coming here, to the other side of the island. The view is different. The water here seems to go on forever." She sighed, looking out on the lake that was so clear beneath her feet, and then turned darker as she looked out onto the horizon.

"I like it for the peace and quiet. Working at the bar day after day... I love it, but it gets old."

"Oh?" She thought of what the girls had said, about Mack's reputation. She would have thought working in a place like Hackney's would be exactly what he craved. New faces every day, never much to feel bored with, or commit to.

"Long nights. Lonely nights," he said, giving her a puppy dog face.

She shook her head ruefully and nudged him with her elbow. "Come on. Let's kick off our shoes and wade in."

He looked at her in surprise but didn't argue. The water was cold but she didn't mind. She was already ankle deep when she noticed him still sitting on the rock, watching her. The intensity of his stare sent a shiver down her spine that had nothing to do with the temperature of the water.

"You mean to tell me that this is your favorite spot on the island, but you don't usually actually get in?"

His grin showed that she'd caught him. "Busted. The water is cold this time of year. Cold most of the year."

She shrugged it away. "It's just water. It doesn't bother me."

"Not much does, I'm gathering," he said with a tone of admiration.

She swallowed hard at the way he seemed to look right through to her innermost feelings. At the way her chest was beginning to pound.

"I'm definitely the most easygoing one in my family," she said. "My older sister is the fretting type. She's a mother."

"Well, that's what mothers do," Mack said with a chuckle. He hopped off the boulder and began kicking off his sandals.

"Not all mothers," Ashley remarked before she could stop herself. Darn it. This was supposed to be a fun, casual day, a little break in the trip, not a chance to get deep. "Sorry. It's just that my mother isn't like my sister. She used to be... but that was a long time ago. My parents split up when I was younger," she felt the need to explain.

"I get it," Mack said. "Mine too. I was always being shuttled back and forth between their two homes, always having to adjust to change. It's not easy."

He waded close to her and Ashley shook her head. "No. It's not. Although in my case, I mostly stayed with my mother while my dad...moved on."

"It shapes you, you know?" Mack stood with his hands on his hips and looked out onto the horizon, but something in his expression told Ashley that maybe he was looking somewhere else, like the past. "I think that's why I jumped at the chance to take over the bar. Make something all of my own. Something that no one could take away, something that was permanent. Life was complicated for me as a kid. But here, it's simple."

He grinned, and darn it if her stomach didn't do a little swoop.

"Life was always better on the island," Ashley agreed, wondering if the simplicity was part of the reason. None of the usual day-to-day stress that wore on a person, or, maybe, a couple. "But life can't be a vacation every day."

"No, but we're adults now. We get to choose a new path for ourselves," Mack said.

Ashley lifted her eyebrows, knowing he had a point. She just wasn't sure if she'd chosen anything, or if, instead, she'd managed to dodge a choice.

"My sisters are very settled in their adult lives, but it was easier for them, being older, already out of the house when the divorce happened."

"What about your other sister?" Mack asked, and she was grateful he hadn't pushed the topic.

"Rachel. She's a therapist. She's very…stoic."

"So you're the emotional one then?"

Ashley frowned, thinking for a moment that he was right, but only then realizing that he was wrong. Or that maybe, she'd been wrong about herself.

"I'm the fun one," she said with a slow smile as she reached down and scooped up some of the icy water, splashing it lightly at him.

"That's why I like you," he said, splashing her back.

Yes, Ashley reminded herself. She supposed it was. They were both two carefree people, him living on island time, her here on borrowed time, both knowing that today wouldn't lead to much. They were living in the moment. And it was enough.

It would have to be.

* * *

Rachel and Lisa were on the porch when Ashley arrived back at the house later that afternoon. Rachel was working on her book, or at least staring at her notebook, and Lisa was frowning down at her phone.

"Do we have service out here?" Ashley wondered aloud as she kicked the stand on her bike. She could have saved herself a trip into town if they did, but then, she wouldn't have run into Mack. And they wouldn't have made a plan for tomorrow.

"No, just checking." Lisa looked guilty when she stuffed the phone back into her pocket.

"Worried about Maisie?" Ashley asked. "I'm sure she's having the time of her life."

"I'm sure she is," Lisa said, but she didn't seem happy about it.

Ashley climbed the porch steps and collapsed on a wicker chair. It creaked from age. "Don't take it personally, Lisa. She's getting older. She won't need you forever, and you wouldn't want her to."

Lisa frowned and then seemed to swallow hard. "You're right, I wouldn't, but...I'd want her to know that I'm always there for her."

"Because our mother isn't?" Ashley pursed her lips. She forced a small smile and reached out to shake her sister's knee. "If I know you, you'll always be there for your daughter."

Even if Lisa hadn't always been there for her. She'd tried, Ashley knew, but then she had Maisie. And Maisie became her entire world. And wasn't that how it should be?

She knew that, but somehow, it still hurt all the same.

A loud sound drew Ashley's attention from the porch as she mounted the stairs. "What's all that noise?"

"Contractor," her sisters said in unison, but it was Rachel who turned to look at her with interest. "Check him out when you get a chance. He'd be perfect for Lisa."

"Stop that," Lisa scolded, shaking her head. "I already told you—"

"What? That you're too old to get back out there?"

Ashley grinned, happy to play along as she dropped into another chair, grateful for the shade after the uphill bike ride had been more exertion than she'd expected.

"If you get married again, you'll give me months more inspiration for my blog."

Lisa wasn't having it. "Talk to Gemma. She's getting married again. You could feature something here, on the island. Your readers would love that."

Ashley considered it. They would. But the problem was that she wasn't going to be here for the wedding, even if she asked Gemma for some details. She'd rely on someone else's photography. And it wouldn't have the same sense of personal experience and anecdotes that her readers craved.

"I imagine the house will be sold by then," Ashley said. It was the first time they'd addressed the actual sale of the house since arriving here. Until now, they'd skirted the topic.

"With any luck," Lisa said, after a beat.

Deciding that she needed a distraction from the strange pull in her chest, Ashley decided to check out this contractor and give her opinion. She walked into the house to see the bottom of a man's feet on a ladder high above her on the second-floor landing. Deciding she could probably use a light sweater for the evening breeze, she slowly went up the stairs and smiled at the man, who stopped working when he saw her.

"You must be the youngest sister," he said, flashing her a grin that showed perfectly straight teeth and a darling dimple.

Ashley estimated him to be in his mid-thirties. Tanned, built, and friendly. Check, check, check. Normally this type of exchange might lead to an invitation for a little banter, but today Ashley's mind was somewhere else. It was still back at the lakefront, she realized. On that rocky shoreline. On that simple kiss that Mack had bestowed on her when they'd parted at the end of the road.

She brushed her fingers over her lips and then straightened her back. "And you must be the guy who's going to make sure this house sells."

"Shame to sell a house like this," he said. "Most people could only dream of having something like this in their family."

Ashley let that soak in for a moment and then gave a small nod. Most people still had a family to gather in a house like this, not leave it to fall into a state of disrepair as they'd done. The house was like another member of the Anderson clan, forced to go off on its own, to be left behind, to do its best against the elements thrown at it.

She wanted to apologize to the house, and she did, silently, as she grabbed her sweater from her bed and then descended the stairs again, with a final wave back at the contractor.

Her sisters were still in their places on the porch when she pushed through the screen door, leaving it to slam loudly behind her. Rachel looked up at her with interest while Lisa looked purposefully uninterested and tended to her notepad instead.

"Well?" Rachel asked with a grin.

"Handsome," Ashley agreed. But not in any way that moved her. She tipped her head at Lisa, giving her a little nudge. "And why wouldn't you be interested?"

"Please," Lisa scoffed. "I have this house to sell. I don't live anywhere near here. Now is hardly the time to be starting anything with anyone."

No, Ashley thought. She supposed it wasn't.

So why did it feel like she was doing just that?

19
LISA

Ellie Morgan was the first person to greet them when they arrived at Sunset Cottage the next night, Lisa, admittedly a little tired from a week of stress and manual labor, and Rachel quiet even for her. Ashley, however, wasted no time in shoving the pie they'd purchased from the bakery at Lisa and sprinting across the lawn and up to the porch stairs to greet her old friend.

Lisa felt a smile pull on her face as she watched the scene unfold. It wasn't much different than when Ashley was nine or ten and the girls would greet each other with squeals and hugs before dashing across the road to the lake as if an entire school year hadn't passed, not to be seen again until dinnertime.

"After all these years, it's like nothing has changed," Lisa remarked once she and Rachel joined the others on the porch.

"Other than Kim not being here," Ashley said, giving a fake pout as she linked arms with Ellie.

"She's a married woman now!" Gemma said, stepping out onto the porch and accepting the pie. "She was married right here on the island. I had to miss it but the pictures were beautiful."

"More inspiration for your blog?" Lisa glanced at Ashley.

"Maybe." Ashley shrugged. "But I'm not here to discuss work tonight, though. But I might pick your brain about your wedding details another time, Gemma."

"Gladly!" Gemma beamed. "It's my second time planning a wedding. But this one will stick. I'm sure of that."

Lisa thought she saw a shadow cross Ashley's face but it was quickly replaced with a bright smile.

"How do you know?" Ashley asked. Then, clearing her throat, she said lightly, "I mean, how does anyone know?"

"I was heartbroken after my first engagement ended, but it was the best thing that could have happened to me because it brought me here, where I met Leo. And after meeting him..." Gemma sighed with contentment. "When you know, you just know."

She said it with such conviction that Lisa wondered if that was true, but then she supposed she was so young and inexperienced when she married Steve, and their circumstances didn't lend much opportunity to second-guessing herself. Sometimes, though, sometimes she wondered if they'd met when they were older, like now, if they would have...just known.

Rachel, who had remained strangely quiet during this exchange, and was no doubt struggling to hold back her professional opinions, stepped forward to give Ellie a hug.

Lisa was the last to greet the youngest of the Morgan

sisters, admiring how tall and beautiful she had become while noticing that the same spirit and energy remained. She still wore her hair in a long braid, like she often did as a child, and there was a gleam in her eyes that always drew people to her. Lisa was pleased to see that so much had remained the same.

"I hear you're quite the artist," Lisa said. "Travelling the world!"

Ellie gave a modest smile but it was clear that she was thrilled by the compliment. "Only because Gemma encouraged me. And because I knew that she would be looking over the house in my absence."

Lisa nodded. She knew from Leo that Ellie had been the one to stick around, stay with her grandmother for many years after college, while her sisters had stayed in Chicago, but she couldn't completely relate to the struggle Ellie felt at leaving the house. It was something that her family had done with far too much ease, she realized with a bit of shame.

And something that now she wasn't even allowing herself to think about. She'd learned through motherhood and maturity that there were some things in life that just had to be done, and when that decision was made, there was no sense wishing for other outcomes.

Like her divorce from Steve, she told herself as she let Ellie and Ashley catch up while she moved on to the table where Gemma was already pouring sangria for Rachel. She and Steve had been at each other's throats for months, even years, maybe. When she thought about all the little arguments and resentments that had built up, staying together wasn't an option.

They weren't any good together, she reminded herself firmly. They were better apart. As friends only. So why did her heart suddenly long for more?

"Sangria?" Gemma asked, holding up a glass.

"Yes, please," Lisa said, shaking herself back to the present.

"Hope you don't mind that it's casual," Gemma said. "If Hope were here, it would all be perfect, of course. You should see that woman throw a party."

Lisa smiled fondly. Hope had been her closest friend here on the island. Like Lisa, she had felt a responsibility to the younger ones, but unlike her, it would seem that Hope's life had fallen into order. Two young daughters. A solid marriage.

"It's a shame that I won't see her when she returns for your wedding," Lisa said. She made a promise to reach out to her when she returned home. She could still find a way to see the people from the island, especially now that she'd found them again. But it wouldn't be the same, would it?

"You could always come up for the wedding," Gemma said. "You don't have anyone renting your house for this summer, do you?"

Rachel caught her eye briefly as she reached for a chip from the bowl on the table. Lisa took a large gulp of the sangria. "That's so kind of you." She tried to think of a polite excuse and failed, and who knew, maybe the house wouldn't be sold by then. Maybe she would come back up for the weekend, or longer.

Maybe she'd bring Maisie with her—she'd be back from

France by then. Maybe this wouldn't be the last time she slept in that old, rambling house after all.

She felt strangely hopeful for about one instant until she remembered what had to be done. She might not like it, but it was necessary. The house was forgotten by her family. Neither Rachel nor Ashley had voiced a desire to return after this, and her mother certainly wouldn't step foot in it. Without that house selling, she'd lose her business. It was very simple when she put it that way.

Except when she glanced over at the big, beautiful home across the grass and everything felt so complicated again.

"Andrea's here!" Rachel said, perking up.

"And that must be the man who won her heart." Lisa turned to see her friend strolling hand-in-hand up the porch steps. Even though Lisa thought Andrea had never looked happier than when she'd seen her the other day, she now knew she was wrong. Andrea positively glowed tonight.

"John Bowen, meet the Andersons," Andrea said, as handshakes went around.

"I feel as if I already know you all," John said with a friendly smile. He was handsome in a classic way, Lisa quickly noticed, a bit older than she and Andrea, but the greying near his temples only made him seem more dignified. Beneath the casual clothing, it was clear that he was a city boy at heart, someone that probably fit in easily at one of those restaurants Rachel liked to frequent that only made her feel like running back to the suburbs and the comforts of her home. But there was a warmth in his hazel eyes and firmness in his hand that made him seem not only sincere but welcoming in a way that she hadn't encountered in some time.

"I can see that you make Andrea very happy," she said.

"More like Andrea makes me happy. I'd just about resigned myself to the bachelor life when I met her. She's changed my world," he said, slipping a hand around her waist.

Was that how Steve felt? Had he resolved himself to bachelor life only to have a woman come along and give him a second chance at love?

"More like you've changed mine. I don't think anyone else could have pulled me away from that promotion I'd worked so hard to finally get," Andrea said, laughing. She took a glass of sangria from Gemma and looked in wonder at Rachel and Lisa. "Sometimes I think about how easy it would have been to have never met John. How if I hadn't come back to the island last summer..." She shuddered.

"Why did you come back?" Ashley asked as the group spread out, making room for the new additions. The porch was large, with ample furniture, and used to housing a group of this size, Lisa knew.

"We came back for summer's end," Andrea said a little sadly, reminding Lisa of the tradition that Taylors had at the end of each summer, to close out the season. "We wanted to honor our mother properly, all together. It was right before the wedding and Kim insisted on it, and I had some time off work and no excuse not to join her. Turned out to be the best thing that could have happened to me."

"Life is funny like that," Ashley said, glancing over at Lisa.

Yes, Lisa thought, it certainly was. If Maisie hadn't applied to that summer program and gotten accepted, then chances were that Lisa wouldn't be here now. She'd have found a way to manage the house sale from a distance. She would have been back in her little town in Illinois, shuffling Maisie to friends' homes and dance classes and to the neighborhood pool, trying to keep her struggling shop alive by day, sharing dinners with Maisie and Steve by night.

Evening Island—the house—and moreso, these people would have remained a firm part of her past.

Only now they were here, surrounding her, laughing and talking, reminding her that life here on the island had continued, even without them.

And it would do so once they were gone, too.

"Penny for your thoughts," Leo whispered in her ear, causing her to jump. He topped off her drink with the pitcher. "Sorry, didn't mean to scare you."

"I was just thinking how nice it is to all be together again like this." She blinked quickly, happy that she'd worn her sunglasses. Across the small gathering of chairs, Rachel was having a deep discussion with John now, something that told her she was likely talking about her practice or city life or both. Ashley and Kim were listening to Gemma's wedding plans. Neither of her sisters looked as emotional or torn as she felt. They were living in the moment, enjoying yet another perfect porch party on Evening Island.

Because that's what every evening on this island as far back as she could remember had been: perfect.

"I was just thinking about how much we've missed out

on, not coming back here in all these years." She gave a sad smile, thinking it was odd that she'd only just really met Leo but that she felt that she could open up to him like this.

But then, Gemma was like a sister, someone who had known her as a child, watched her grow, and was there for the foundation of her life. She wasn't just a friend, she was family, and so, by extension, was Leo.

"No sense in worrying about the past when you could be enjoying the present," he said kindly. "Besides, you have more time in front of you than behind you."

Lisa tried to smile as she watched him make the rounds, topping off everyone's glass before settling into a seat near Gemma. It was true what he'd said, echoing what her sisters had been trying to say even if she hadn't wanted to hear it. She didn't spend enough time looking to the future.

But she hadn't really preserved the best parts of her past, either.

"Not when it comes to this island," Rachel remarked and then, catching Lisa's warning glance, cleared her throat. "I mean that I'm leaving. Tomorrow."

"Already!" Ellie shared the same disappointment as the rest of the locals, and Lisa quietly did too. She could technically stay another three weeks until Maisie returned, but with Rachel leaving, the house would feel more empty and...different. And she wanted to remember it the way it was.

"I'll probably be leaving next weekend," Lisa said with a sigh. "We have lives to get back to."

And an entire life to leave behind, she thought, suddenly struck by the fear that she might burst into tears at any moment. She took a shaky sip of her drink and gave a brave smile to Ashley, whose expression was unreadable.

Ellie leaned over to whisper something to Ashley, which brought her usual smile back to her face.

"Ellie's going to show us a painting she did," Ashley announced, distracting everyone from the darkening mood.

Ellie, looking a little embarrassed at being cast into the spotlight, went into the house and returned a moment later with a large canvas, its back to the group.

"It was just something I did while I was on the road."

"Something from Paris?" Lisa said, only to blush when she caught Rachel's sharp look. Of course, she had France on her mind. How couldn't she when her daughter was there, right now, doing who knew what?

"Or Italy?" Ashley volunteered. "The seascapes must have been so inspiring!"

Ellie gave a funny smile. "Actually, it's one of Evening Island. I know that I must have a hundred paintings of this place, but even though I was taking in new sights, traveling to countries that I'd only ever dreamed of visiting, when I sat down to work, the one place that I kept picturing was...home."

She carefully turned the canvas around so that it was facing them. A collective sigh went up in the group. They'd all seen endless paintings of the island, of course; it was impossible to spend much time on the island without passing the gallery or gift shop windows that proudly put so many on display. But this wasn't just a painting of the island. It was a painting of this porch. This very same wicker furniture. Nine little girls all curled up in various positions and stages of activity.

There was Lisa, braiding Hope's hair, while having her hair brushed by Andrea, and Gemma, her legs curled up, reading a book. Heather and Rachel were scribbling in notebooks and Ashley and Kim Taylor were dancing. A younger version of Ellie stood at the base of the porch, painting the very scene they were looking at now.

"What do you think?" Ellie asked, looking a little nervous. "One of my usual shops in town might take it but—"

"It's priceless," Lisa said, as she realized just how true that was. Any shop would be lucky to have it, but no one who bought it would understand its true value.

Ellie must have thought the same thing because she extended her arms in Lisa's direction. "Take it. Please," she said.

"Oh, I can't!" Lisa shook her head. "You worked hard on this. You should sell it!"

"I have others to sell, but this one... This one belongs to you. Take it with you when you leave. To remember us all by when you're not here."

Lisa really feared she might cry now and she stood up, carefully taking the painting with shaking hands.

"I'll treasure it," she promised.

"I know you will." Ellie smiled. "And seeing how happy you are to have it is what gives it meaning."

And wasn't what something meant to the recipient what mattered more than anything that could be picked up in a shop? Lisa thought about that as she sat down again, carefully holding the painting in her lap, away from the table where it could be stained or ruined.

But when she looked back up at all the familiar faces surrounding her, she thought of something else. Something even more impossible to forget.

That somewhere along the way, she'd gotten everything wrong.

20
RACHEL

Rachel stared at the open suitcase on the floor of her bedroom and heaved a sigh. Usually, packing was something she did with pride and tackled with a reliable system that made her never worry about forgetting something. She usually made a list—as early as a month out—and then set everything aside in the days before the trip. This time, she'd done none of that.

The clothes she'd worn all week had not been washed, much less folded and set in neat piles, ready to be tucked into the suitcase that would transport them back to the condo on the Gold Coast. Her toothbrush was still resting nicely beside the faucet in the bathroom, along with her other products, which had not been stuffed into their bags to avoid spillage.

There was no list. There was no plan. But there was one glaring thing: denial.

The day had arrived, as she knew it would, but she had not prepared for it. When she closed her eyes and tried to picture herself walking through the lobby of her co-op building, waving to the doorman, stepping into the elevator, and then, eleven floors up, her apartment, she felt like she was watching someone else's life unfold. Because when she thought of what felt right, natural, and where she wanted to be twelve hours from now, it was not in that sleek, spotless apartment in the sky. It was here in this creaky old house, specifically out on the front porch with her sisters, a glass of wine in her hand, a stack of cards on the table, the lake breeze in her hair.

It was crazy to think this way. She knew it. But was it crazy to go back, now, when so much was still unresolved? She'd come here to clear her head, but all she'd done was escape her problems. She wasn't ready to face them yet.

Rachel narrowed her eyes on her suitcase and then walked to the small desk near the window, where her planner was tucked under the laptop, for extra height. She pulled it out now and leafed to this week, cringing only slightly when she saw all the plans she'd canceled, and next week, which was a bit light, meaning she could stay, if she really wanted to. It wasn't ideal, but life wasn't always as neat and tidy as she wished it to be—and she knew that.

Or rather, she should have.

With a pounding heart, she set the planner on her laptop and left the room. Downstairs in the kitchen, she could hear the sounds of pots clamoring, and Ashley and Lisa in lively conversation, talking about the plans for the house.

"Oh, you saved me!" Ashley said dramatically when Rachel came into the room. She stood at the stove, stirring eggs. Beside her, a cutting board of freshly chopped vegetables was waiting. "Lisa wants to get up into the attic today, and you just know there will be spiders up there."

Rachel didn't point out that she'd seen a spider in her bathroom just an hour ago. Instead, she smiled, relieved for the distraction. "I can go up with you if you need help," she offered to Lisa.

Lisa turned from the sink where she'd been filling a vase with water, a look of surprise filling her face as she reached for some freshly picked peonies, which grew later in the season this far north as opposed to back in Chicago. Not that Rachel grew flowers on her balcony. But she did take a jog through Lincoln Park every morning of the week, so she'd learned to notice these things.

She noticed a lot. Always had. But she hadn't noticed what was right in front of her, had she?

"Aren't you leaving today?" Lisa walked the vase to the kitchen table and set it in the center.

"I think I'll stay, actually. Wait and drive back next weekend with you. It beats renting a car and... The dinner last night made me realize how much we've missed out on here. And if it's our last time all being here on the island, I don't see any rush in saying goodbye."

A silence filled the room for a moment, and Lisa fiddled with the flowers, even though they were perfectly cut, arranged, and centered on the table.

"Marty won't mind?" Lisa eventually asked.

Rachel struggled to make eye contact and instead walked to the cabinet to get a coffee mug. She prepared her cup slowly, hoping that her voice would remain measured.

"Marty is usually gone most of the week anyway, and he

and I have always been independent. It's how our relationship works." Or so she'd thought. Now she realized that instead of leaning on each other, instead of sharing each other's lives like she'd thought they were doing, they were just circling each other's orbits. Other than a charity event or a social obligation, they lived completely separate lives. Ones built on mutual respect, sure, but not ones that were intertwined.

Lisa gave her a funny look but then shrugged. "If it works, it works. I guess it's different when you have kids. You have to be in constant communication."

Feeling her temper rise at the judgment in her sister's tone, Rachel took the bait. "Is that why you and Steve still spend as much time together as you did when you were legally married?"

"We do not!" Lisa's mouth firmed. Ashley's eyes went wide as she gave a dramatic wince. "We have the occasional dinner together. With Maisie. As a family. I don't think there's anything wrong with getting along well with my child's father. It definitely beats the alternative."

That was true, and already Rachel felt bad for bringing it up. This wasn't about Lisa or Steve or their marriage. This was about Marty. And Rachel. Because she'd played a part in things too.

Somewhere over time, a lack of communication became normal, comfortable even. But was it normal for her and Marty to go for five days each week without seeing each other, much less not checking in, or having a conversation?

It wasn't any more normal than the fact that she hadn't checked in with Marty since she'd been here, and that other than sending a brief text today when she could catch a signal, there would be no need for further explanation. Marty wasn't the type to say he missed her or wanted her to come home any more than she was.

But that hadn't meant she hadn't missed him, hadn't looked forward to Friday nights when she heard the door to their apartment open. Hadn't wanted to suggest he catch an earlier flight or cut back on the meetings. But she couldn't. Because that wasn't their arrangement. That wasn't what worked for them.

Except that what she'd thought had worked hadn't in the end.

Taking a breath she said, "Anyway, I'm here for another week."

"Well, that's great!" Ashley was the one to break the silence. "You can crawl up into that dusty attic."

"And what will you be doing today?" Lisa asked as Ashley turned to reach for a plate.

Their younger sister's cheeks turned a bright shade of pink, and Rachel glanced at Lisa, sharing a small smile.

"Let me guess. You're going out with that handsome bartender," Lisa said.

"He actually owns the bar," Ashley said, and now her cheeks were positively flaming. "And it's just a little fun. That's all."

"You sure that's all?" Rachel didn't believe her for a second. She plucked a peach from the fruit bowl, and after a brief pause where she calculated that Lisa would have most definitely washed all the produce before setting it there, took a juicy bite.

"Of course that's all!" Ashley bristled and took an extra plate from one of the high cabinets. "That's all there ever can be."

"Because we're selling the place," Lisa said, looking a little troubled.

There was a beat of silence before Ashley nodded firmly. "Exactly. Because soon, I'll be gone, never to return. And all of this..." She swept her hands over the sunny kitchen. "This will all just be a memory."

* * *

Rachel was sitting on the front porch reading a novel she'd found on one of the shelves in the sunroom, trying not to feel guilty about leaving her patients for another week, when she spotted Ray coming up the road. She watched as he carried his tool chest, assuming that it was heavy, with ease that certainly didn't reveal it.

"Howdy," he said, giving her a grin as he approached.

"It must be hard to be a contractor around here. No cars."

He shrugged. "I like to walk. Besides, you can't beat these views." He turned to admire the lake across the road and Rachel did the same.

She let out a sigh of contentment. "You're right. I almost feel guilty for keeping my head in a book all morning."

"Eh. It's Sunday."

"And you're working," Rachel pointed out.

"Good excuse to come to the island." Ray grinned as he came up the stairs. "What are you reading?"

Rachel was reading one of those steamy romance novels that her mother liked to indulge in only when they were here at the summer house, always careful to tuck them away on the weekends when their father came up on the ferry, not that he would have probably noticed. Their father was all business, more concerned about an upcoming trial than his wife's pastimes. Now, Rachel realized how little they'd had in common.

It was one of the reasons she'd been so confident when she'd accepted Marty's proposal. They were two of a kind. A perfect match. They were, she'd dared to think and maybe even believed, unstoppable.

"Oh, just...something to pass the time." She turned the book facedown, but she felt heat creep up her cheeks all the same.

Ray was on the porch now, giving her a knowing grin that was so adorable she wished Lisa could come outside and see it for herself. Maybe it would convince her to take her eyes off her ex-husband for a moment.

"My sister reads those books. Buys them in a cute little bookshop in Blue Harbor."

"I'll have to check it out sometime," Rachel said, even though she knew that she wouldn't have the opportunity. Once they were on the island, there was a silent understanding that they didn't leave until the end of summer—or in this case, until the end of the trip. Somehow, doing so would be like a magician showing his hand. There was something so special, so all-consuming about being here, away from the cars and the noise, and the small things that made up everyday life, that destroying that feeling, for even a moment, would somehow tarnish the entire summer. Make them remember that there was an entire world waiting for them across the water. A world they weren't ready to get back to just yet.

"So, Lanie tells me you're all planning to sell this place." Ray looked up at the porch ceiling, possibly for further examples of damage, or maybe just out of idle curiosity, or appreciation. There was no denying that these homes on West End Road, with their lush gardens and sweeping views, were something to treasure.

And here they were about to just give it away—or at least that's how she'd come to think of it. The thought of selling it to the highest bidder made her stomach hurt, and made her feel like all those happiest parts of her childhood were up for grabs. It wasn't like she needed the money from the sale.

Lisa, on the other hand, seemed to be focused on just that.

"None of us ever get back here very often, and renting the place out each season has been, well, a burden on my sister." She frowned now, wondering if that were true, even though Lisa had used those words, or at least hinted at them. "It's a big house and we're not such a big family anymore. My parents don't ever come up, so..."

She trailed off, worrying that she was talking too much, but Ray just looked at her with a pleasant smile and interest in those striking blue eyes. Because there was no other word for them. They were striking. And strangely, very warm.

"My parents divorced when we were teenagers and we stopped coming up. This is actually the first time that my sisters and I have all been back."

He gave a frown of compassion. "Too many bad memories?"

She thought about that for a moment and then, to her surprise, smiled and said, "Too many good ones." She laughed. "That probably doesn't make any sense."

He took a step closer and set his toolbox on the porch rail. "Oh, I think it does. Sometimes, it's harder to look back on all the good moments you lost. Sometimes, it's easy to focus on the bad so you can move forward."

She wagged a finger at him. "You're in the wrong profession. Anyone ever tell you that you'd make a good therapist instead of a contractor?"

"I'm just a good listener is all," he said with an easy smile that made Rachel's heart beat a little faster. "When I'm with good company."

"Well, I am a therapist," she said. "And I'm afraid that even I can't make myself feel completely right about selling this place."

"Sometimes it takes someone else wanting what you have for you to realize how much you still want it." He chuckled. "I had this old car that always needed work, the thing was more trouble than it was worth, but it was my first car, and it was a classic. I saved up for that thing, tinkered with it, and kept it running. When that thing broke down for about the hundredth time, I decided that was it. Listed it for sale, and got three offers the same week. Hearing people talk about all its good parts made me, well, it made me want to cry."

He made a puppy-dog face to show he was joking or at least exaggerating, and Rachel burst out laughing. "Tell me you didn't."

"Oh, I did. Sobbed like a little girl." He grinned again then stepped back. "Nah. It's in the garage, under a tarp. I don't drive it so much, but I couldn't say goodbye to it either. It's not practical, but it's special. And more importantly, it's a part of who I am."

Rachel pulled in a breath and nodded slowly. This house was a part of who she was, a part of all of them. If she stared at the lawn long enough, she could almost see a younger Ashley speeding up the hill on her bike, tossing it down onto the green grass, and then running barefoot up the stairs, her hair sweaty and sticking to her forehead, her cheeks a bright pink and her eyes shining. Her mother would be sitting in the biggest of the wicker chairs—her favorite—shaking her head and attempting to reach for a cloth napkin to wipe the dirt from Ashley's cheeks, before finally tossing up her hands and laughing.

She had the best laugh—when she laughed. It had been so long since Rachel had heard it that she'd nearly forgotten the sound. Until now.

Rachel didn't even realize she was smiling until she caught Ray looking at her. It was a look of appreciation, not judgment, and something in her stiffened when she caught herself.

"Anyway, it's not really my decision to make. It's my sister's, Lisa's." She eyed him carefully, wondering if the name would spark a reaction. It didn't. "She's the pretty one who called you."

A polite nod was his response to that.

"She's been in charge of the place, and it's a lot for a single, unmarried woman." She waited, but again, Ray just gave a pleasant smile and a tilt of his head to show that he was still listening.

"Well, old places like this take work and something beyond what's in this chest." He tapped his toolbox.

"Oh, and what's that?" Rachel asked, genuinely curious.

"Love," he said with a wink.

Now, Rachel's heart was absolutely pounding, and she was relieved when he picked up the toolbox and, with a little salute, pulled open the creaking screen door and disappeared into the house.

If she didn't know better, she might just think that he wasn't interested in Lisa after all.

That maybe, he was interested in her.

21
ASHLEY

Ashley debated between cut-off jean shorts and a cotton sundress, then grumbled to herself for overthinking it. This was a date, and a casual one, a daytime one no less, and besides, what did it matter what she wore or how she looked? She knew the rules. She'd created them. There was only today. Maybe another. Not much beyond that. Certainly no future.

She should not be getting caught up in silly things like what to wear.

She reached for the dress because it was already proving to be a warm day without a cloud in the sky.

Her sisters were on the porch when she appeared a few minutes later. Rachel, with a book she recognized as one of their mother's favorite summer escapes, and Lisa with her long list of home projects, which she had to have memorized by now.

It saddened her to see how much time her sister was putting into the house instead of enjoying the time that was left in it, but then she supposed that was the entire point of this trip. Meeting Mack, getting out and having a little fling —that had certainly not been planned.

"Well, don't you look pretty!" Lisa looked up from her notepad as the bang of the door signaled her arrival.

"It's just an old cotton dress," Ashley said, instantly regretting her choice when she saw the way her sisters both regarded her with amusement. "It's not like this is a big deal or anything. Mack's a nice guy. He asked me to join him for lunch. It's nothing more than that."

"If you say so," Lisa said with a little smile.

"It's not like that," Ashley insisted, feeling her defenses prickle.

"What's wrong?" Lisa blinked up at her. "I thought you liked him."

"I do like him," she said simply. Because that part was easy. It was everything else that was complicated.

"So, what's the problem then?" Lisa said with a shrug.

"Well, for starters, he lives here, on a remote island. And do I need to remind you that we're selling this house?"

Ashley saw the look her sisters exchanged and realized that her tone was sharper than she'd intended.

"Sorry. I just...get tired of people asking when it will be my turn to walk down the aisle. The more weddings I go to, the more people want to know."

"You do go to a lot of weddings," Lisa said gently. "And you do run a blog based on those experiences."

"Exactly," Ashley said. "Other people's weddings. Not my own."

"I never realized you were so against the idea of

marriage," Rachel said, lifting her eyebrows. "You fooled me right along with your readers."

"That's not fair," Ashley said. "Besides, you don't really know me, Rachel."

As soon as she saw the hurt in her sister's eyes, she regretted saying anything. This wasn't like her—first agonizing over what to wear for a casual lunch and then getting all annoyed when her sisters teased her.

"You're my little sister. I remember things about you that you probably don't even remember about yourself."

Ashley knew she could let it go, apologize, diffuse, flash a smile and change the topic, which is what she usually did. But something about this day had fired her up. She was anxious. About her future. About what she was doing with her life. What was next.

All this time, she'd thought looking forward was easier than looking back, but now she wasn't so sure of that. Or anything, really.

"It's been a long time since we've spent any time together. And a long time since we've talked."

"We're talking now," Rachel said.

"You know what I mean," Ashley said. "And actually, I'm surprised that given your profession you haven't recognized that already. Anyone can talk. But really talking, knowing someone, well, that takes time and effort."

"And vulnerability," Lisa said, nodding. She glanced at Rachel, whose expression had gone completely blank.

"I know that we're not close anymore," Rachel finally spoke. "I'd hoped our time here would fix that."

"Really?" Ashley had to stop herself from laughing out

loud. “Because you’ve spent most of your time here sitting upstairs in your room, alone.”

“I’ve been working on my book,” Rachel’s tone held a defensive edge, not that Ashley was surprised. “And if you recall, I was all but banned from helping out with the house projects.”

“You weren’t banned,” Ashley said with a roll of her eyes.

Rachel gave her a knowing look and Ashley had to grin a little. “Maybe a little banned.”

“I’m happy to help!” Rachel said, turning to Lisa.

“I know you are,” Lisa said softly, but she hugged the list a little tighter to her chest.

“It’s not just that. You’ve been hiding out. And...you haven’t worn your wedding ring since we got here,” Ashley countered.

Lisa’s eyes popped and she quickly picked up her pen and scrutinized her notepad.

“I took them off the first night to shower. I guess I just forgot to put them back on,” Rachel said evenly.

Now Lisa was looking at Ashley from the cover of her lashes. A light had flicked on, but Ashley wasn’t so sure that she wanted to know what was inside Rachel’s head. Or if it was even any of her business.

Ashley could feel a headache coming on, and she wondered if there was any ibuprofen in the house. If there was, it was probably left behind from over a decade ago. Expired. And unsafe. Just like this island. It opened up memories, old wounds, and hurts. And she didn’t want to hurt her sister tonight. She loved her sisters.

Even if she didn’t know them anymore.

"I don't want to fight. We don't have many days left here. We should make the most of it. I'll be back in New York soon. We'll all go back to our lives. Everything will go back to the way it was."

There was a collective murmur of agreement, but like her, neither Lisa nor Rachel looked pleased with the thought.

"I'd better get going," she said, reaching for the porch rail.

"Me too," Rachel said, standing. She looked down at Lisa. "That book won't write itself. You coming inside?"

"I think I'll sit out here for a bit before I head up to the attic." She gave Ashley a smile of consolidation. "Hey, have fun today, promise?"

Ashley grinned, feeling the weight leave her body. She never liked arguing with her sisters. She'd only ever wanted them to be close.

"I will," she said. Because that was one promise she could keep. To her sister. And to herself.

* * *

Today, Mack's idea of fun wasn't a picnic on the lakeshore. Or a restaurant, which was what she'd sort of been expecting. Instead, Mack invited her back into the kitchen at Hackney's and handed her an apron.

She looked at him in alarm. "We're cooking?"

He laughed. "Don't tell me you can't cook."

"No, I can," she explained. "I just don't have a chance to do it very often in New York. My kitchen's about as big as a doormat. Maybe a bathtub."

He laughed again. "And you like living there?"

Despite the shine to his eyes, the question was serious, and one that she'd never really considered before.

"It's not permanent," she said slowly. "But then, what really is?"

He gave her a strange look as he reached for a pan. "I like to think that this place is permanent. I wouldn't be committing so much to it if I didn't believe in it or really want it."

"Do you plan to be an islander forever?" She marveled at that. Summering on Evening Island was one thing, but only a few hundred Michiganders lived here year-round. Winters were harsh, especially without cars or easy transport, and access to the mainland was difficult when the ferry stopped running.

"I'd like to travel. I have a rainy-day fund." He grinned at her. "But it's nice to know that I'll always be to come back to a place I like. I have a business I'm proud of, one that everyone enjoys. I can do my thing, on my terms. And isn't that the point of life? Spending time doing what you like, with people you like?"

She gave him a little nudge. "Anyone ever tell you that you're too smooth?"

"Smooth, sure, but too smooth?" He looked at her, his expression turning a little more serious. "So I'm known as a bit of a flirt. What can I say, I like to have fun. I like to enjoy life."

"A man after my own heart," she said, then, catching the way his eyebrow cocked on that statement, she blushed.

Moving over to the sink, she busied herself by washing

her hands. Still, she was pleased to sense Mack's gaze on her the entire time.

He handed her a cutting board when she moved back toward him and motioned to a bowl of tomatoes. One was already sliced.

"I mean it, though. Is New York where you're putting down roots? Is it the one place on earth that you feel you can't live without, that you'd be heartbroken to never return to again? That makes you feel...like you're exactly where you're supposed to be?"

She chewed her lip, hoping to override the pain that tugged in her heart. She'd never thought about it before. Never questioned it. She'd moved to New York because all of her sorority sisters had after college graduation. It was a natural choice, but that didn't make it the right one.

"I guess that if I had to name the one place on earth that makes me feel like I'm exactly where I need to be, it would be...here."

His gaze was intense as he gave a little nod. "A girl after *my* own heart then," he said, inching toward her.

I'm not sure I even have a heart, she thought, even as it began to beat quickly, reminding her that it was there. Bottled up, denied, forgotten about much like that dusty old house up on the hill, aching to come alive.

Mack was looking at her with that lazy grin that probably made dozens of girls swoon and shouldn't be more than a passing interest to her, except that something had changed, something that she couldn't control.

She knew that now was the time to abort the mission, to

make up an excuse and end this date. To never see him again. To disappear. This was her cue to exit.

Except this time, she didn't want to run. She wanted to stay right here. In this kitchen. And she wanted him to kiss her. Not just for a bit of fun or someone to fill the emptiness. Right now, there was no emptiness. Her heart felt full, like it might actually burst. It was a hard and steady drum inside her.

Mack stepped forward, closing the distance between them, and pushed a strand of hair out of her face. The gentleness of his touch sent shockwaves through her in a way that no other kiss or touch or connection had, and she wasn't exactly shy when it came to dating. It was all the other stuff that was new—the heart-pounding emotion. The anticipation. The need.

Everything in her mind was telling her to get out—now! But her eyes closed as his face neared and his mouth met hers, softly, tenderly, and she leaned into his kiss, letting him wrap his arms around her waist, pulling her tight against his hard chest, making her wish this moment would never end, even though it would.

All things did.

But this... She pulled back, giving him a small smile, trying to make sense of what had just happened. It was just a kiss, she told herself.

But it was some kiss.

He resumed his task, giving her little sidelong smiles that made her heart kick each time, and she did the same, went back to work, slicing the tomatoes with a shaking hand, taking her time so she wouldn't ruin the day by hurting herself, even though she feared that was exactly what she was doing. What she'd set in motion by coming here today, by returning to this island at all.

That was the hard part about loving where you were or what you did. If it didn't work out, or it was suddenly taken from you, then heartbreak was inevitable.

And she couldn't have that.

22
LISA

Lisa knew she'd be on her own when it came to cleaning out the attic, but she didn't mind—well, except for the dust. Climbing up the stairs on Monday afternoon for another round of sorting boxes and thinking about what items could be moved downstairs into the house for a better showing, she sneezed three times before hitting the top, her eyes watering as she weaved her way through boxes and old furniture covered by tarps toward one of the windows, praying that it wasn't sealed shut like half the others in this old house.

With plenty of grunting and a fair amount of resistance, she managed to pry it open, grinning at how sometimes the smallest of tasks could be the most satisfying.

With the light coming in, the old space was almost cheerful, and, overlooking the dust motes that lazily floated through the air, Lisa tackled the boxes she hadn't gotten to yesterday, only to see that they, like the others, were unlabeled. Their mother hadn't packed up this house—old Edward probably had, years and years ago, at their mother's instructions. He wouldn't have known how to label each of the girls' things or even whose room was whose. She'd be lucky to see each room packed up together, rather than mixed in together.

But she had time. And she liked this sort of task—it helped to keep her busy, to have a purpose, to feel like she was being useful. It made her feel like she was taking action in getting the house sold, even though the more she went through the old memorabilia, the more difficult it was beginning to feel to part with it.

But rummaging through old things was a pastime, possibly one that was born in this old house, because she'd always taken an interest in the items left over from when her grandparents had been the ones to occupy it, always carefully examining each "dust catcher" as her mother called them, wondering where it came from and what its purpose was. As she grew older, her interest only increased and she eventually came to realize that not every object in a house needed a purpose other than to evoke a special sort of feeling or a memory.

Not so long ago, when she and Maisie would sit around, dreaming about their trip to France, they would talk about the flea markets they might visit, and the treasures they would find. It was why she'd called her shop The Treasure Box, because each item in it was unique, carefully selected, and presented in a way that should make the recipient or owner feel like they had something special in their possession. It was the hunt for these types of objects that gave Lisa a thrill, and, if she was being honest with herself, helped keep her mind focused on more positive things.

And today, rummaging through these old boxes would help keep her mind on her purpose for being here. And off what was going on back in the small town that she shared with Steve.

Had the date been a one-off or turned into more? Either way, it felt personal, directly related to her even though she knew that was ridiculous. Had the woman ever come in the shop? Lisa pondered this while she glanced through the contents of a large but rather light box (beach toys that were faded from days of being left out in the sun and probably should have been tossed a decade ago—or more). Imagine if she had, if Lisa had met her, even liked her. Or maybe she hadn't liked her. There were always a few each month, people that would say things were too expensive, or return something they'd been given as a gift, not willing to take store credit even though they didn't have a receipt.

What if they got married and started a new family? What if Maisie became a sister to a child that Lisa wouldn't even know? Maisie had grown used to the shared Christmas mornings and Thanksgiving dinners with both of her parents present. Lisa had too.

Now, Lisa's stomach dropped on that thought as she pulled the tarp off a tall object, revealing the free-standing mirror that had once been in their parents' bedroom—passed down from their mother's grandmother, they knew. Too precious to be left out for renters who wouldn't necessarily respect its value.

Lisa looked at her reflection and looked away, not liking the frown she saw as she strategized whether she should contact an antique dealer here on the island or consider selling the house furnished. The real estate agent had said they'd want to keep their options as open as possible, and getting a household of furniture to the island wouldn't be easy. But not every piece would need to be included. If it were easier to bring this back with her, she'd take it for herself, but that wasn't an option, and it could be worth hundreds. Maybe more. It could pay for a month of rent at the store. Buy The Treasure Box another fall. Get her into the holiday season, when sales peaked again.

But then where would she be come the spring? There was a deeper problem with the store than bringing in customers who were actually in the market to buy something.

And if she wanted to hold on to it, she'd have to figure out exactly what that was. And soon.

* * *

"Look what I found," Lisa told her sisters that evening, when Ashley had returned from town, a little earlier than expected, and a little quieter than usual too. She'd gone through most of the boxes, sorting the belongings by each sister, along with her mother's pile. She only realized when she'd taken stock just how little of her father had ever been in this house. Sure, he'd only come up for weekends, but not one summer tee shirt remained, no bathing trunks, not even a bottle of his favorite cologne.

She extended the stack of notebooks in various bright colors that had faded with time, still amazed that after all these years, they'd survived. The pages were a little warped and yellowed, but everything was legible, at least from what she'd flipped through.

"Our old journals," Rachel took the one on top from her hands—once a bright blue now more of a greyish color.

"I remember these," Ashley gingerly took the pink one and inspected it for cobwebs, no doubt. "Mom made us write in these things every year."

"I didn't mind," Lisa said, opening the yellow one even though she'd already done so upstairs before, just like now, closing it quickly.

"I loved it," Rachel replied.

Ashley shot her a look. "You would."

Rachel's grin turned sad. "Now I'm glad we did it. I can't believe that she kept them, though."

"There was another one," Lisa said, holding up the fourth journal, this one not a solid color, but instead a swirling mix of watercolors. "Mom kept one too."

"She did?" Rachel blinked at her, clearly as surprised as Lisa had been. "Did you read it?"

Lisa shook her head. "I just opened it to the first page to see what it was. I saw her handwriting." She swallowed hard. "It's been a really long time since I've seen her handwriting."

"Mom's not exactly a letter writer," Ashley said softly, but there was a hint of sadness in her voice.

"Or a card sender," Rachel agreed. "Though neither am I."

Lisa held the notebook out, but neither of her sisters took it. Instead, they all seemed to inch backward, as if they were afraid to get too close.

"I never saw her write in it." Lisa tried to think back on

the hundreds of days that had been spent here in this house over the years.

"What should we do with it?" Ashley asked, giving her one of those looks that she'd grown used to seeing on Maisie's face, one that told her that she needed help, and direction, and she didn't quite know how to ask for it.

"We don't have to decide that now," Lisa said.

Rachel nodded firmly. "I agree. Let's set it aside. We can decide if we want to send it to Mom."

"Do you think she'd want it, though?" Ashley looked alarmed at the mere thought. "She never even talked about this place after...well, you know. That last summer."

Lisa was quiet. That last summer had been blissful, full of the usual activities that they'd come to take for granted, assumed were a guarantee that started each June and ended each August. There was the first ferry ride over, the unloading of the many trunks, the airing out of the house, and the quest for provisions. There was the lugging of the bicycles from the carriage house, checking their tire pressure, grinning as they climbed onto their seats and pedaled into town, inhaling the rich, almost overly sweet smell of fudge that mixed with that clear air that seemed to fill their lungs so much more than their apartment in downtown Chicago could ever do.

There was the first morning, when they woke up to the sunlight streaming through their linen curtains, the first breakfast, which was usually rushed and harried. The first jaunt across the lawn to find their friends, who all arrived more or less the same week, and that first dip in the lake, even if it was always icy cold at first.

Eventually, the days blurred together. Long and lazy, with evenings that seemed to go on forever, even well past sunset, which happened later at this location in the time zone. Well past their usual bedtime. But here there were no rules, not really. Except one. To keep these journals. To write in them at least once each week, every summer.

"She might not want it," Rachel said.

Lisa stared at the book, seeing that it was worn, that the spine was loose, and that the pages were likely filled.

"Well, she entrusted me with this house and by default its contents. I'll hold onto it. Mom might want to bury this house and all its memories in her past, but that doesn't mean we have to do that."

There was a shifting of feet as the sisters fell silent. They knew what they were all thinking. That by selling this house that's exactly what they were doing. Cementing it into their past for good. Eliminating any option of ever returning to or revisiting that special moment in time. Of acknowledging that that part of their lives was behind them, permanently, and ensuring that they could never, ever go back.

"I think I'll take a shower before dinner." Lisa glanced at Ashley. "Are you going into town tonight?"

"No. I'm staying right here with my sisters. That's the entire reason I came on this trip. Meeting Mack was just...a fluke."

Lisa was touched by Ashley's words, but regret reared hard and deep. "I'm glad you decided to stick around a little longer, Rachel. I'm glad we have this time."

Rachel gave a small smile and then smoothed her ponytail. "Well, it's not fair to let you handle it all on your own, even if we are here mostly for moral support."

"And errand running. And nutrients." Ashley quickly pushed back her chair. "I thought I'd make us a pasta salad. I recently learned a new recipe. Maybe some berries and cream for dessert?"

"That sounds really nice," Lisa said. Because it did. Because more and more, everything about being here in this house felt nice. Like it always did. But it was more than that. It felt right.

23
RACHEL

Rachel hadn't looked at her so-called advice book since she'd made the decision not to return to Chicago on Sunday as planned. Instead, she'd read her mother's old romance novels, smiling each time she came to a dog-eared page, wondering what might have pulled her mother's attention away from the book enough to set it down. Ashley with another scraped knee? An unexpected but always welcome visit from Mrs. Taylor or Mrs. Morgan?

Rachel had never been one to demand much attention. She was too quiet, too self-assured. Now, she supposed she could trace it back to her birth order as the middle child, but she knew it was also just her nature. She lived in her head.

But lately, her mind wasn't the best company. It made her doubt not just her book and the advice she was giving to her patients, but everything else.

Even this old place.

She was sitting on the porch with a glass of lemonade,

reading the third book in what must have been one of her mother's favorite series, listening to the pounding on the roof. Normally, this type of disruption might have bothered her, but she found it comforting instead, reassuring to know that someone else was close by, especially when she couldn't be sure about her sisters' whereabouts, though she had her hunches about Ashley, who was no doubt spending a little more time with that bartender.

She flipped a page in her book, blushing a little as the scene unfolded on the page, wondering for a moment just what Marty would say if he saw her reading it when, other than the occasional thriller, normally the newspaper or an industry journal occupied her nightstand or the glass coffee table in their painfully uncluttered living room. He'd be equally appalled at all the knickknacks collecting dust for no purpose in this old house, she assumed.

She nearly smiled at this when she realized that the pounding had stopped and that someone was close by. Dropping the book, she jumped a little to see Ray standing halfway up the porch steps, looking a little sheepish and a little like the man on the cover of the book; well, at least his chest did.

"Sorry. I thought I could sneak into the house for my toolbox without interrupting you. You looked so peaceful there."

Rachel dropped her feet from the wicker loveseat she'd been occupying for the better part of an hour. Ray used this time to grab a handkerchief from the back pocket of his jeans to mop the sweat from his forehead. Feeling strangely intrigued by the gesture, she tried to glance away by shoving the book between the weather-worn cushions.

"It's fine! Really! Can I offer you a lemonade? It's fresh." She stood up, resisting the urge to stretch even though her legs sort of ached. "Well, from a powdered mix. Still, I made it just this morning."

He gave a slow grin that made her stomach uncoil. "Well, in that case, how can I resist? Artificial is my favorite kind."

She looked at him skeptically. "Really?"

He laughed. "I'm afraid my jokes aren't winning you over."

Her cheeks flushed with that, and even the ice in her glass could do nothing to help. "I'm afraid that I'm considered the serious one of my sisters. I take people at their word. Even when I probably shouldn't."

She hesitated, thinking that she'd done just that with Marty. Assumed that he'd meant it when he said that he wanted the same things as her—even when she wasn't so sure that she wanted that herself.

"Every family needs a straight man." Ray wiped the remaining beads of sweat off his brow. In the few days he'd been here, his skin had bronzed from the sun exposure, making his eyes even bluer, almost electric.

And she was staring.

"And who would that be in your family?" Back in her comfort zone, she relaxed.

"My older sister. I used to joke and say I had two mothers growing up, the way she doted on me. Scolded me sometimes too."

Now Rachel laughed. "Well, my older sister, Lisa—" She

paused again, waiting to gauge his reaction, but there was none. "She's only a couple of years older than me, so no chance of that. But she's definitely the nurturer, and my younger sister relied on that for a while."

She waited to see if he would seize the chance to comment on Lisa, but instead, he just stared into her eyes, grinning that grin until her breath caught.

"I'll go get that lemonade." With a pounding heart, she darted across the porch and pulled open the screen door, letting it bang behind her, something that would have made her mother reprimand her if she were here.

But her mother was not here, and never would be again. And besides, Rachel was a grown woman. A married woman, at least technically. Legally. And Rachel played by the rules. Rules kept life tidy. Rules kept things from falling into chaos.

"Get a grip," she hissed to herself, standing at the kitchen sink. She took three steadying breaths and then opened the cabinet for an extra glass, remembering what Gemma had said about the pattern on each, smiling when she realized she was holding the one with the lilacs. She added a heavy amount of ice, topped off the glass with the lemonade, and closed her eyes for ten short seconds before deciding that she was being completely ridiculous.

Ray was sitting on the porch steps, facing the lake, when Rachel returned.

"Oh, you're an angel," he said, taking the glass from her. "I ran out of water an hour ago."

"You should have come into the kitchen and helped yourself!" Rachel hesitated, thinking it would be a little odd to return to her wicker chair now. Instead, she took her glass from the table where it was resting and then moved back to the porch steps, taking a seat as far to the edge as she could, leaving almost enough space that she couldn't quite smell the damp sweat coming off that, well, incredibly toned body.

Ray caught her glance and grinned. Stiffening, Rachel took a long sip of her lemonade. When it was gone, she'd make an excuse and go back inside. She did have a book to finish, after all.

"I wouldn't want to intrude. You ladies have enough going on, what with the sale."

Just remembering that, Rachel felt her stress replaced with something more like sadness.

"This house has been in the family for generations. I hope my great-grandmother won't haunt us after this."

Now it was Ray who peered at her before the corner of his mouth slowly lifted. "Ah, a joke. I knew you had it in you."

"You don't think I'm one of those types who believe in the supernatural?"

He looked at her frankly. "No. I think you are far too level-headed for that."

"But you hardly know me," Rachel said lightly.

Ray took a sip of his drink and looked out over the water. "Oh, I think I'm a pretty good study of people. And I've been around enough these past few days to pick up on a few things."

"And what is that you've gleaned?"

He glanced at her sidelong, his grin telling her that he wasn't so sure she wanted to know. Still, she laughed, playfully nudging him with her elbow. Catching herself, she scooted another inch to the right. She was now pressed up against the wooden rail, at risk of getting a splinter, no doubt, but it was a risk she would take. It beat the alternative.

"Well, your younger sister, Ashley? I think she might have her heart set on the guy who owns Hackney's."

"You noticed it too?" Rachel leaned in. "Of course, she won't admit it."

"And your other sister. Lisa?"

Rachel's breath caught for a moment. She wasn't sure why, but suddenly, the thought of Ray having an opinion on her older sister worried her. Somehow knowing where Lisa stood once and for all would make all of this a little clearer.

"She's always trying to get cell reception. Every time I see her, she's holding up that phone, searching. Something tells me that's she's searching for more than just a connection to the outside world."

She tipped her glass in his direction. "You, my friend, are very insightful."

"Oh, so we're friends now, are we?" He grinned, and darn it if she wasn't now staring at those perfect white teeth.

"Of course. Summer friends. That's what I always used to call the people here on the island. We picked up every June right where we left each other in August, and even though nine months would go by, another year of school, and another round of adventures to share, it was like no time had passed. There's something about this island that makes time stand still."

Now it was Ray who was staring at her, and she wondered if she'd overshared until she saw the softness of his gaze.

"That's what makes it so special," he said softly.

She looked straight ahead, to the water, where a sailboat cut through the soft waves in the distance, leaning into the wind. "It is special. I feel like I sort of took it for granted all those years we'd come up here."

"Your parents don't ever come back?"

Rachel shook her head. "They got a divorce when I was a teenager. The property is technically my mother's, but she's made it very clear that she wants nothing to do with it."

"My parents split up when I was a kid, too. Probably why my sister felt the need to look out for me."

"Sisters are good for that sort of thing," she said lightly, only then realizing how true that statement was.

Her sisters were good people—so different than her that it was almost hard to believe they were biologically related, but still, they had her back. They supported her. Loved her. Didn't ever really question her.

But maybe because she'd never given them a reason to doubt her. Because some part of her was afraid of what would happen if she let her guard down, let them in. If she'd lose another person she cared about. A dynamic that she'd treasured as much as she'd pushed away.

"Well, I should get back to work. That roof won't fix itself, I'm afraid." He pushed himself off the steps and stood, giving her a full view of the length of him, from the faded jeans to the tee shirt that seemed to make every muscle in his arms and torso only more obvious.

Rachel stood too, more abruptly though, looking out over the water, having the strange desire to run over to it, shed her shoes, dip her toes in. And—even crazier—ask Ray to join her.

"Wouldn't that be nice if it could?" Rachel said wistfully, knowing just how much the cost of these repairs was worrying Lisa.

"Oh, I wouldn't say that," Ray said slowly. "Then we wouldn't have had the opportunity to have these nice chats."

Rachel grinned. They were nice chats, and for once, it wasn't her doing all the listening.

With disappointment, she took the empty glass from his hand, stiffening when their fingers brushed for a second, nearly causing her to drop the glass. But she couldn't drop this glass—this glass was the lilac glass. The best of the set. It had survived years of use, spills, and even renters. It had been used by her mother when she was young, by each of the girls when they were too.

And soon, it would be left behind—or maybe tossed out as nothing but an old piece of glass—forgotten about forever. As if it never existed.

Frowning, she held both glasses a little tighter and walked toward the door, eager to return them safely to the kitchen, to wash and dry them and put them in the cabinet where they would be safe. Where they belonged.

Something hit her before she got that far, though.

"Hey," she said, forcing him to stop and glance over his shoulder. "You never told me what you've been observing about me."

His grin turned mischievous as he picked up his toolbox. "We'll just have to save that for another conversation."

Another conversation. Rachel tried to hide her smile as

she stepped inside the house, knowing that she should leave the glasses in the kitchen and get upstairs, to her desk and the book that was waiting to be finished. But she couldn't focus on that just now. She was thinking about how nice it was to talk to Ray, and how much she was looking forward to doing it again.

24
ASHLEY

The next day when Ashley headed out to see Mack, she tried not to think about how many days she had left on the island, even though that's exactly what she'd been doing since she'd come back. She was saying goodbye at the same time that she was reconnecting, and this time, like the last, she knew exactly what she missing.

Only before, there was always a distant, vague hope of someday returning, even if it was never discussed and the years passed by.

She knew Mack was working most of the day and night, but she'd decided to pop in, sit at the bar before it got too crowded, and have a drink before she headed home for dinner. She told herself that it was because she really needed a break from all the redecorating and furniture moving that Lisa was doing, and it was...because the more that Lisa fussed with the house, the more attention she gave it, and the more she felt attached to it. But the truth was that she also wanted to see Mack, hear his laugh, hear her own laugh when she was around him.

So long as she knew the rules and kept to them, then there was no harm in that, she told herself.

It was still early so she decided to poke around in some of the gift shops in town, to see if something caught her eye that she might want to bring back with her to New York, even though her apartment could do without any additional things. Already it was cramped, with the lone closet stuffed from floor to ceiling, the small space under her bed, too, and all the clever organization tricks she tried didn't seem to make the space feel any more practical, much less inviting.

Maybe that was why she didn't use it for much more than a stopover place. Why she didn't feel a longing to return or a connection or any emotion at all when it came down to it.

Or maybe it was more—more like what Mack had said. It was just a small square box with a single window. It wasn't her home. But what was?

She wandered through a home goods store, thinking that this was really more Lisa's type of place than her own—all too grown up and settled for her taste, not to mention impractical for her living situation—before moving back onto the sidewalk. The ferry boats were visible through the gaps in the shops across the street, making their way over to the docks, carrying more tourists who would soon flood the candy shops and stationery stores and fill the streets with their rented turquoise bicycles and wire baskets filled with their purchases.

Ashley moved on to the next storefront, realizing from

the printouts taped to the windows that it was a real estate office. Skimming the listings of homes ranging from waterfront condos near the harbor to small cottages tucked in the woods, she wondered if Lisa had seen this yet. The prices were steep but wide-ranging, and the inventory was plentiful if someone was looking for a summer place, the season that pulled most people here to the island.

But living here year-round was different. She'd never experienced winter on the island and tried to picture it now. The horses clomping through the snow. The Christmas tree set up in the middle of town, just like in that one painting of Ellie's.

She studied the listings with interest, seeing a couple that could compete with their own cottage, though none on the coveted West End Road, of course, with its walking distance to town and prime location just footsteps from the lake and access to the big hotel, which had put this remote island on the map.

There were other listings, too. Ones here in town, for cozy apartments over storefronts, their rents almost laughably affordable compared to what she was paying in New York.

She mused on this as she stepped aside to make room for a young couple, whom, from the way they pointed and looked, were more browsers than buyers, like her.

Of course like her. She righted herself. She wasn't seriously considering living on this island, was she? She had her own island. One with millions of people. One that never grew quiet, even in the middle of the night. One that was never dark. One where she never felt alone.

Or so she'd thought.

Walking down Main Street, a thought started to form—or maybe it was more of a daydream. A fantasy as ripe and beautiful as the weddings she attended. One that was just a glimpse of an idyllic version of life, not the harsh reality of it.

She could picture herself, walking this street, getting her groceries from the limited selection at the Main Street Market, spending the winter months tucked inside her apartment, leaving only to frequent the spots that would all be walkable, of course, as everything on the island was. Coming together much like they had all those summers ago when the island itself was their bond, their shared experience, something that the rest of the world couldn't understand. Seeing Gemma and Billy and Andrea and Ellie and Heather...

And Mack.

She could do it if she wanted to. Her work allowed for that, and there would be plenty of weddings on the island to cover. Maybe over in Blue Harbor, too. Gemma's, for sure.

She could do it. The thought repeated itself over and over, as she approached Hackney's, there on the corner, where the windows were opened and the crowd was already visible and everyone was laughing and having a good time.

She could do it, she thought, as she opened the door and walked into the room. And when Mack looked up and grinned at her, and her heart sort of dropped into her stomach, she knew that she did want to. And that nothing was stopping her but herself.

* * *

Hackney's was more crowded than she expected it to be at this hour, but Ashley's disappointment was recovered when Mack made space for her at the bar by finding an extra stool and dragging it over to the end.

Did she notice the narrowing of the eyes of the women on the opposite end? Who wouldn't? But she wasn't here to gloat or to feel like she'd won something. She was here to spend time with a man that she liked. A lot.

Maybe, too much.

"What'll it be?" Mack spread his arms wide on the bar top and gave her a waggle of his eyebrows that sent her heart a flutter.

"Just a glass of white wine," she said a little breathlessly. "I'm having dinner with my sisters tonight."

"Family bonding?" He lifted a bottle of sauvignon blanc from the fridge under the bar and poured her a glass.

"More like a family tradition," she said slowly, thinking of how many nights they'd spent on that porch over the years, even in the rain. It was like another living room of the house. The best one, really.

"Well, don't drink it too quickly. It's shaping up to be a long night and you're the friendliest face I've seen all day."

She knew he was just flirting, but she couldn't help but blush. "Aw, I bet you say that to all the girls."

"Just you," he said, holding her gaze.

Ashley swallowed hard as her chest began to pound. Feeling shaky, she gave a tentative smile. "I think I'll give my hands a quick rinse first."

She walked to the bathroom with too much noise in her head, too many thoughts and warnings going off like alarm bells. It was like that weekend with Michael—only worse. Because this time it wasn't someone wanting more than she could give. This time she wanted something she couldn't have.

Or could she?

She let herself into the room, happy to be alone for a moment, and turned the tap on warm, running her hands under the water until she could get a grip on herself. But no matter how much she talked herself down, her heart kept lifting her up.

She was the one who had made the rules. And she alone could change them. She was her own person; the choice was hers. She could go back to New York, to the same routine that had become comfortable, safe even, or she could try something else. Take a risk.

Fill that part of her that had remained so empty for so long because for so long that's what felt better. Now, it just felt like what it was. A void. A denial of everything she ever was and wanted to be and wanted from life.

She glanced up into the mirror, seeing a strange light in her eyes that she'd never noticed before—or maybe hadn't been there until now.

A light that had faded a long time ago, along with the cries of joy she'd left behind on West End Road, the little girl who'd run through life at full speed, savoring each day, enjoying each moment, never worrying about tomorrow.

Well, she didn't have to make any decisions today. But there was a decision to make, she realized. For the first time in so long, she was tempted.

With a strange sense of hope, she pulled open the door

and strode down the hallway, taking her time, feeling that sense of joy and purpose, and direction. Mack was at the bar, another man leaning over where her empty stool was wedged near the opening, laughing at something that Mack was saying.

Pausing, she decided to let them finish their conversation, but her heart sped up when their voices became more clear.

"Yep, that's me," Mack was saying. "Never the same girl in my life for more than a season."

"A season." The other man snorted. "More like a fraction of the season. This place is a revolving door to more than just tourists."

Mack gave a wry grin and tossed the bar rag over his shoulder. "You know how it is on the island. People come and go. There aren't a lot of people here year-round."

"And would you want it any other way?"

"Heck no." Mack's grin broadened, and Ashley felt her own smile fade.

She should have known—in fact, she did know. She'd heard it from everyone, all the women she knew and trusted, all the ones who cared about her. Mack was a player and a flirt and he took life in stride. That's what she'd liked about him. That's what had made him safe.

And that was why there could never be anything more between them. Even if she wished there could be.

Decision made. Even if it was made for her. Again.

Squaring her shoulders, Ashley walked back to her stool and slapped a twenty-dollar bill on the counter. Mack looked up in surprise. "You're leaving already?"

"Yep." She managed a tight smile but the shadow that

passed through his gaze made her realize that her emotions were pushing through to the surface—and she'd always been so good at keeping this from happening.

"You okay?"

"Of course!" she said brightly. "Why wouldn't I be? I'm here on the island, where life is fun and easy and a total escape from the real world across the water. Who couldn't be happy here?"

"You'd be surprised," the other man laughed. "Some people complain about the smell of the horses."

She managed a shallow smile. "Well, I'm calling it a day. Bye, Mack."

They locked eyes for a moment and she knew that he understood. She was saying goodbye. To tonight. To tomorrow. To the possibility of any day after that.

"Wait." Mack stopped her before she could get very far.

Reluctantly, she stopped and turned to face him, hating the confusion she saw on his face. Wishing that she'd never let it get this far. Every other time, she'd managed never to let it happen, but somehow this time had been different.

He picked up the bill and held it out. "I can't take your money. It's my treat. On the house."

"For your rainy day," she said, thinking back to the conversation they'd had just a few days ago, the one that made her feel like she knew him in a way that others didn't. A way that made her feel connected.

She hurried out the door and around the corner, eager to get back to the house. Back to the house that she thought she'd never bear to part with again, after just reconnecting it. Back to the house that she now knew with certainty needed to be sold. Needed to be gone so that it was no longer a part of her life at all, no longer a reminder or a temptation. Along with every other part of her experiences on this island.

And like most everything else about the old family lake house, that hadn't changed with time.

25
LISA

Lisa had spent all day putting the finishing touches on the house—from moving select objects and pieces from the attic to adding vases of fresh flowers from the yard. Now, she stood back nervously as the real estate agent made the rounds, nodding while she quietly observed the rooms and took note of the repairs.

"You made some changes to the décor," Lanie said.

Lisa grimaced, even though she saw it as an improvement. "I was cleaning out the attic and I found all these things that...used to be here." She motioned to the pillows on the couch, the vase on the mantle, and the books that she'd carefully arranged on the shelves. "I guess I just wanted to make it feel more like the way I remember it."

"It looks better," Lanie praised. "You want a buyer to have an emotional response when they come through the door. You want them to walk inside and immediately feel like this is somewhere they want to live. More importantly, somewhere they can't live without."

Lanie's smile felt stiff as she looked around the space that had slowly been transformed, everything put back in its proper place, no longer cleared out for renters but filled with all the special objects that had been a part of their family.

"I'm afraid it still won't be a quick sale," Lanie explained when she finally stopped walking and turned to face her.

Lisa tried to recover from her disappointment, but she worried that she wore it on her face. It was something she'd always done, unlike Rachel who could keep her features so even that Ashley used to tease her she should give up her practice and turn to the poker tables instead.

Sure enough, Lanie set a hand softly on her arm. "It's not impossible. But selling a house of this value is never easy. There are only so many buyers looking for properties at this price point."

"I understand." Lisa sighed heavily. She'd never be able to afford this house—neither would her sisters, or even her parents. It wasn't lost on her that she was parting with something of enormous value.

And not just monetarily speaking, she thought, looking over at Ellie's painting, which now hung over the mantle.

"Have you had any inquiries?" Her heart was pounding when she looked at the real estate agent, willing her to give her some true hope, but knowing in her heart that there probably was none.

"Not yet." Lanie's tone was bright, maybe even optimistic, but she didn't understand that time was of the essence. This wasn't about just parting with a piece of their family estate. This was about solving a problem. And a big one.

Just then, there was a knock from the hallway, and Lisa stepped to the side to see Ray's figure behind the screen door.

"Oh, Ray, you here to finish up?"

He grinned as Lisa held the door for him, and he stepped inside. "Should be all finished today. Then nothing can stop you from selling this house. Isn't that right, Lanie?"

"Ray." Her cheeks flushed. "Well, you've certainly put the pressure on me."

"Oh, now. Just calling it as I see it." He tapped the banister when he looked at Lisa. "You have a good real estate agent here. And a solid house."

"And are you in the market?" Lanie cut in, but even Lisa didn't hold her breath. She couldn't decide if Lanie was being sharp or just plain flirting.

Rachel was right. Ray was a handsome man, with bright blue eyes, a friendly grin, and a taught body, tanned from hours on the job.

But he wasn't Steve. And that was just the problem.

"Wish I was, but a house this size is probably better suited to a family. And the means to keep it going."

A family. Only she'd never brought her family here, had she? She'd kept the house, telling herself it was so she could pass it down to Maisie one day, but now she realized that was just a lame excuse. Maisie was busy each summer, with her own interests: dance camp, art camp, or just spending time with her friends at the lakefront near their house. And Lisa had gotten busy too, fallen into a new life and a new routine.

She'd held on to the house for the family she used to have, back when she was just a girl. And she'd finally thought she could let go of it now that she wasn't that person anymore.

But a part of her still was. At least here, in this house.

Pulling herself from her thoughts, Lisa nodded. "The upkeep on a place like this isn't easy. At least there are great people like you to help out with the job."

She instantly dropped her smile. What was she doing? Flirting with this man?

She caught Lanie's narrowed glance, confirming just that. She could practically hear Rachel's thunder of applause from her room upstairs, where at least she was luckily tucked away behind a closed door, none the wiser of this particular misstep.

Ray, at least, didn't seem to notice. He lifted his toolbox higher and mounted the first stair. "Well, I'll leave you to it. Lanie, nice seeing you again."

"Very nice," Lanie said, clearing her throat. Her gaze followed him for a moment as he ascended to the top floor and then she lifted her chin and seemed to snap out of that when she suddenly turned to Lisa. Her smile was again warm. "I'm pleased with what you've done with this place. It feels homey and loved. That will certainly help sway anyone who is on the fence."

"If we can even get anyone to consider it," Lisa said, feeling her anxiety heighten.

"That's my problem, not yours." Lanie tipped her head. "You've done all you could. Now, enjoy your time on the island, keep things working and tidy, and wait for my call."

Lisa tried to process what she was saying. "You mean, I could leave the island?"

"I have the key," Lanie replied. "And Ray said he's finishing up today. I don't see any reason for you to have to say."

Lisa was still thinking about this long after Lanie had walked down the porch steps and disappeared down the dirt road, past the three Victorian homes with their large front porches and the sweeping view of the dark blue water.

She was free to go. Eventually, if Lanie was as successful as she believed her to be, she would be free of this house altogether. There was nothing more for her to do. Nothing more that she could control. The outcome was out of her hands.

Nothing was stopping her from going upstairs, packing up her things, and boarding the evening ferry. Getting in the car and driving all the way back to Chicago. From sleeping in her own bed tonight, taking a hot shower with reliable plumbing as early as tomorrow morning.

Except for something. Something that she couldn't identify, or tap into, at least not completely. Something that she didn't want to admit, maybe. Something that, if she didn't know better, she might say frightened her.

And for that reason, she decided to keep this last bit of Lanie's conversation to herself. What her sisters didn't know wouldn't hurt them—if anything, it would hurt them more to leave now when so much had been said and yet not spoken. When they'd just finally come together, for the first time in years, and for what might just be the last time, at least here.

They'd be saying goodbye to this island and this house soon enough. There was no reason to rush it.

And really, what was there to get back to, other than a

failing store and an empty house, full of memories of its own that she didn't exactly care to face just now.

She went around to the side of the house and pulled her bicycle from the carriage house. She didn't know where she was going, or what the end goal was—not for this afternoon. Not for the future. Every once in a while, when she met a curve in the road, she lifted her phone, searching for a signal, for some contact with Maisie. With Steve.

With the people she couldn't stop thinking about, especially when they were far away. But Maisie was busy, as she should be. No news was good news. And Steve—it was time to stop thinking about Steve. It had been time, many years ago.

Tossing the phone into the wicker basket that was coming slightly loose from the metal handles, she increased her speed until her legs hurt and the air filled her lungs. She went through the forest, knowing that few tourists came up this way, and out to Forest Bluff, with its towering hedges that made the houses behind them feel like something out of a storybook. She didn't stop pedaling until she was suddenly on West End Road again—and she realized that she'd come full circle, and she didn't even know how long she'd been gone. Forty-five minutes? An hour? It was possible to take a lap in a shorter time, but she had meandered, instead of moving forward with purpose. And wasn't that the problem?

Unable to go back inside the house and face the reality of her efforts, she propped her bike against the front of the house and crossed the road to the lakefront, where she kicked off her shoes and waded in, the icy cold water a sharp contrast to her warm skin.

She bent down until her fingers grazed the surface, and only then did she notice the drops that landed on the water, rippling out into a circle.

She was crying. She had been for some time.

Heavyhearted, Lisa sank down onto the rock and gazed out over the water, feeling the breeze merge with the tears that streamed down her cheeks. Once, she would have called Steve, but now she couldn't even do that—and not just because she doubted there was any service at this exact point on the island. Steve had moved on. She'd lost him. Twice, in a way.

Just like this house. Just like so many other things that mattered so much to her, even if she didn't realize it until it was too damn late.

26
RACHEL

If Rachel was going to be leaving Evening Island for the last time this Sunday, then she figured she couldn't go without a stop by the Harborside bar. As a kid, it had always seemed so elusive and trendy, with its open-air windows looking out over the harbor. Each summer, when she'd arrive on the ferry with her mother and sisters and suitcases almost too heavy for her to carry, she'd stare through the windows and admire the people and think that someday, when she was older, she'd be one of them.

Trouble was, their summers had come to a grinding halt before she hit the legal age limit. Now, as she wrapped her hand around the cool brass handle and gave it a good tug, her heart leaped a little. It was childish really, a thrill from a time gone by, but it was exciting nonetheless. A feeling that somehow, against all odds, she'd made it. Achieved another life goal, however silly.

The bar was decorated with antiques from the furniture to the wallpaper to the paintings. It was crowded, as it always appeared to be, and she took in the tables, a little more rugged looking through her adult lens, or maybe just from the passing of time. The drinks menu was written in chalk on the board over the bar and she studied it even though she knew that she'd settle on a glass of wine in the end. She wanted to take it all in, memorize it perhaps. She owed it to herself.

"Will it be a Saddle Sore or a Runaway Buggy?" a deep voice, that was strangely familiar, said from close by.

She glanced over in surprise to see Ray leaning back in his chair at a high-top near the open windows, the lake spread out behind him, with the Michigan coast not too far off in the distance, but far enough to make her remember that she was somewhere far away, somewhere physically separated from the rest of the world. And her troubles.

"This is the first time I've seen you here," he said with a grin and motioned to the empty chair across from the small round table.

She hesitated only a moment before hoisting herself onto it as gracefully as one could in espadrilles and a skirt that was probably better suited for her office back in the city.

"This is my first time coming here, actually." She grinned as a college-aged waiter appeared and she gave her order. Ray ordered another beer for himself, which pleased her more than it should. It was the prospect of his company, she supposed. The relief of not having to sit here alone. She could have asked one of her sisters to join her, but they wouldn't have understood what the place meant to her. How could they? It was a strange little aspiration, one that she'd written about in the pages of her journal on that first crossing each year.

"I come here a lot," Ray admitted. "It started off the first time I had to wait for a ferry. Now, whenever I come to the island to do work, I look forward to it before getting back to the mainland. There's something about this island that makes you resistant to going back to regular life. And this place...it just seems to embody what I like most about the island."

Rachel held her breath, realizing that he was voicing her exact sentiments, something she'd tapped into even as a teenager who already longed to grow up, and who did, much too soon.

That something about this place drew her here. That maybe, if she dared to believe such things, it might be Ray. It might be...fate.

The waiter appeared with their drinks and she took a quick sip of her glass and then another. Ray was grinning at her, but his eyes were questioning.

"Everything okay?" he asked.

Boy, he wasn't wrong when he said that he picked up on things in people.

Rachel gave a breezy shrug and set down her glass. She watched a ferry in the distance for a moment, confirming just how far the mainland was. "My sisters claim I have an unreadable face. What makes you sense that something might be amiss?"

Ray's eyebrows shot up but he leaned into the table, which wobbled only slightly, accepting the invitation for deeper conversation.

"For what it's worth, I don't think you're hard to read. I think you're...reserved. I think you wear your feelings close to your vest."

"You would be right," she said, and for a moment she didn't know whether to be impressed or scared. No one had ever seen through to the real her before. Not her parents. Not even her sisters.

Definitely not Marty.

Just thinking about him dampened her mood so she tried not to, but it wasn't that easy.

The volume of the music picked up for a minute, pulling her attention away from those encroaching thoughts. She glanced at Ray sidelong. "It's like the roaring twenties in here," she remarked.

"Exactly." He grinned and set his beer down and she realized as he stood that others were doing the same. "It's five o'clock. It's happy hour. And here, that means you dance."

She automatically stiffened. Dancing was something she did not do. Didn't know how to. She envied people like her sister Ashley who could flail themselves around without a care, laughing and moving until they were out of breath.

Her gaze flicked around the room where sure enough a few people were swinging their hips to the old-fashioned music, but most were sitting and watching.

She didn't even dance at her own wedding. Well, she hadn't exactly had a real reception, but that had just made it easier. She'd been off the hook.

With a strange jolt, she wondered if there was ever a time that she'd actually danced with her husband, in all these years.

But now Ray was looking at her with a twinkle in his eye and he curled his fingers toward him, teasing her. "Come on. You can't make me dance alone. I've been sitting here every day watching all these other people enjoy this music you only ever really hear on this island, and I've never had anyone to dance with until you walked in and saved me."

Saved me. Rachel felt a strange sensation, because that was what she'd always considered herself to be: someone who helped people, who saved them. But what she didn't realize until now was that she had been the one who needed help. And Ray was offering his hand.

"I'm not very good at this," she grumbled as she slid off her stool, adjusting her skirt.

"It's not a competition," he said with a laugh. Then, moving close, he said in a low, husky voice, "And I don't judge."

Rachel forced her body to move to the beat, even though it seemed to resist her every intention. Ray, on the other hand, moved with ease, and perhaps sensing her struggle or inner horror, reached out a hand and put it on her waist, until she fell into step beside him.

"See? You've got it."

"That didn't take very long," Rachel said, pleased.

Ray's gaze was intense when she looked up at his tanned face. "Sometimes things just fall into place quickly."

Her heart hammered as the music faded and the room seemed to stop and Ray leaned closer, his lips parting as their faces neared, and a part of her, a deep, lonely part of her, wanted nothing more than to lean into him, to pull him close and enjoy this moment to the fullest.

Instead, she pushed back against his chest, ending the kiss as quickly as it had started.

"I—I can't do this." She blinked quickly, feeling disoriented as she fumbled for her bag and glanced toward the door.

The confusion in Ray's face cut her—shamed her, really—but she couldn't say or do anything at this moment to make him feel any better. She was in the business of helping people, and instead, she'd gone and hurt them instead.

"I'm sorry, Ray. But—I can't. I just can't."

Before he could object, she pushed her way out of the bar and out into the evening air. She glanced over her shoulder, making sure that Ray wasn't following after her, and fought against the urge to go back inside, to sit down, explain, and make it all right. But how could she even do that?

Tell him that she was a married woman when she wasn't even sure she had a marriage to return to? Tell him that she didn't see him that way when somehow, she did?

Or maybe to tell him that she was sorry. For not being honest. With him. Or herself.

And maybe not with Marty.

* * *

Her sisters were sitting on the porch when she arrived home, and she felt her defenses loosen their grip at the sight of them.

"Did you have a nice time in town?" Lisa asked casually, clearly oblivious to what Rachel had been up to, today, and these past few days, maybe.

"Yes," she started, and then stopped herself. It would be so easy to give a stiff grin, claim she was tired, and head up to her room.

But that wouldn't make her feel any better, or less lonely. And it certainly wouldn't make her closer with her sisters.

"Actually, no."

Her sisters turned to each other in surprise, and then Ashley scooted over on the wicker sofa, patting the empty place with an encouraging smile. "Then come sit. I've got time."

Time. It was the one thing that they didn't have really, at least not here, on this porch, or on this island. It was the one thing that was so easy to take for granted when one day poured into the next, and you just assumed tomorrow would be no different.

But time had slipped away somehow, and her little sister was now all grown up, and as much a stranger to Rachel as she was to her.

"I saw Ray."

"Ray as in the roofer Ray?"

Something about the way Lisa said that made Rachel smile a little, in spite of herself. "Roofer Ray, yes. He was in town, waiting for his ferry, and we had a drink, and..." She swallowed hard. "He kissed me."

"What?" Ashley's eyes went wide.

Lisa, however, looked more concerned than curious. "Doesn't he know that you're married?"

"It never came up," Rachel said, even though the truth was that she hadn't brought it up. Hadn't shared that one part of her, when she'd been so able to open up about so much else.

"And you haven't been wearing your rings," Ashley said softly. She gave Rachel a knowing look. "You don't have to talk about it if you don't want to, but...is everything okay with Marty?"

Rachel licked her bottom lip and pulled in a big breath. This was the moment when she could say that of course, nothing was wrong with Marty, that she'd done as she'd already insisted, forgotten to put her rings back on.

But these were her sisters. And much as she might not have opened up to them, maybe, deep down, they did know her. Not what she put out there or wore on the surface, but they knew her heart.

And instead of trusting them enough to open up to them, she'd talked to Ray. Because it was easier. And maybe, because he didn't know her at all.

"Marty and I...I think we're growing apart. I think...I think he could be having an affair."

"Marty!" Lisa gasped. "But you two are so...perfect for each other."

"On paper." Rachel sighed. "I thought so too. Now, well, now I'm beginning to think that we messed up, that we didn't make time for each other. Didn't listen to each other. Or communicate."

"But you're like, a professional listener," Ashley said, looking confused.

"And when I didn't hear any complaints, I made the mistake of thinking there were no problems." She shook her head. "I was so blind. So caught up in my own life that I didn't think about our life. I didn't make time for him. We didn't make time for each other. And now..." She tossed up her hands. "Now Marty appears to be spending time with some blonde who has a better figure than I do." She gave a laugh that held no amusement and realized with panic that her eyes had filled with tears.

"Oh, honey." Lisa reached forward and took hold of her hand, squeezing it tight and leaving it there. It was such a simple gesture, one with little words, but one with full understanding. And a clear message: she wasn't alone.

"What do you think is going to happen?" Ashley asked, then held up a hand to correct herself. "I mean, what do you want to happen?"

"I want to start over," Rachel said, blurting the first thing that came to her, even though she hadn't had the time to stop and think, to analyze it. She realized with a shock that this was what she wanted, it was the first thing that had come to mind, without pretense or planning, or hedging her risks. It was what her heart wanted. "I want to go back to the beginning and do things differently. I want...another chance."

"Oh, honey." Lisa blinked back tears and this time it was Rachel who gave her hand a squeeze. "We all do. At least, I do."

"Me too," Ashley said quietly. She glanced at Lisa sharply. "Wait. Are you talking about Steve?"

Now Rachel couldn't help but laugh and released her hand to help herself to a sip of Ashley's wine. "Of course, she's talking about Steve." She gave Lisa a more sobering look. "You still love him, don't you?"

Lisa dropped her hand and sighed. "I've never stopped. I was mad at him. We were fighting and we weren't getting along. We were both so focused on what we'd sacrificed instead of what we had. We were both so young and money was tight and everything in life felt overwhelming. But he's the only person who shared the journey of raising Maisie. The only other person in the entire world who loves her as much as I do. He understands it. He understands me. We've grown up together. And we've learned from our mistakes."

Rachel took a moment to let that sink in. Why was it that by the time that you realized how much something mattered to you, it was when you were on the brink of losing it?

She looked up to the porch roof and over to the water, feeling a lump rise in her throat.

"Anyway," Lisa said, slumping back in her chair. "It doesn't matter. Steve's moved on."

"He's seeing someone?" Ashley looked so disappointed for her sister that Rachel felt something in her chest pull.

That deep down, despite all her words to the contrary, her little sister was a romantic.

And somewhere along the way, Rachel had become the cynic.

"I think so." Lisa tossed up her hands. "It was bound to happen. He's handsome and still young, and we're not married. We're just...family," she said sadly.

"You are," Rachel said firmly, drawing a look of surprise from her sister. "I was wrong to tell you to move on. I thought that it would be best for you. That it was the only way to move on from the divorce, but I wasn't listening to what you were really saying. And love isn't that simple."

And she should have known that.

"Neither is family," Ashley sighed.

"I think...I think that we all had this picture of what the perfect family should look like and that once it was shattered, we stopped thinking we had one at all instead of making the best of our circumstances." Rachel knew lots of broken families, of course, and most recovered after divorce. Why hadn't they?

"We had so many idyllic summers here in this house," Ashley said, answering her question. "I guess that if we were older and saw more, we might have seen that it wasn't all so perfect. How could it have been if it suddenly ended so badly?"

"Maybe it wasn't sudden at all," Lisa said. "Maybe it just seemed that way to us."

"Maybe, Mom and Dad were trying to protect us from their problems," Rachel said, feeling ashamed that she hadn't thought of it sooner.

"It just felt so abrupt. Never coming back to this house." Ashley brushed away a tear. "And now that we've spent time here again, it will feel almost worse to leave it again, because this time we know...it's the last time."

Lisa was silent for a moment. "When I said I wished I could start over, I didn't just mean with Steve. I meant with everything. I had so many dreams and plans and I kept pushing them off! I pushed off that trip to France and now Maisie has gone without me. I pushed off coming back to this house, even though I kept telling myself that someday I'd take Maisie and I never did."

"But you were the one who wanted to sell," Ashley pointed out.

"I know." Lisa blew out a breath. "My store isn't doing well. Well, that's an understatement. I'm probably going to lose the store."

Rachel was startled. "Why didn't you say something?"

"And have you offer to write me a check or something?" Lisa shook her head. "It's not just about the money. That store means something to me. It's the new life I built for myself when Steve and I split up. It was...my future. And now it's going to be another part of my past. One more thing I've failed at."

"Small businesses go under all the time," Rachel pointed out.

"I know," Lisa sighed. "But I guess I thought...I guess I hoped..."

"That this time it would be different? That something might last?"

"Nothing lasts, though," Ashley said, taking her wineglass back from Rachel.

Rachel watched her carefully, realizing that her sister was hiding her own heartbreak, that for years, she'd been hiding from all of them.

"This house lasted," she said firmly. "And it will even after we're gone."

When this seemed to offer little consolidation, Rachel tried harder. Speaking her own emotions wasn't comfortable, but it was what she expected from others. It was what people needed, herself included.

"And we've lasted. You, me. Lisa." She smiled at her older

sister. "Look at us. Here together. This time we won't lose that again."

"I want to believe that," Ashley said, brushing away a single tear.

Rachel looked out over the water and took in the view that never failed to leave her breathless. She wanted to believe that too.

27
ASHLEY

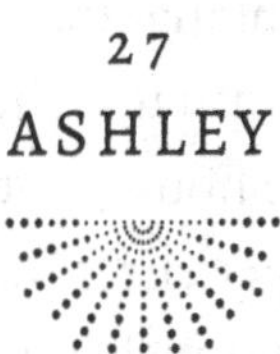

They spent the entire next day making rounds of the house, sweeping the porch and washing curtains, weeding the rest of the flower beds, and polishing every object with a new kind of care. The real estate agent would be coming by to take photos of the interior the next day. Their time in the house was coming to an end.

They didn't stop working until evening, when, freshly showered, they gathered on the porch with a simple pasta dish and a fruit salad.

"I might call it an early night," Ashley said, knowing that she wasn't good for conversation these days. Her heart felt heavy for more than just the thought of losing this house. She didn't look forward to going back to New York. Maybe she never had.

But that wasn't it, not all of it, at least. She'd lost something these past two weeks. A dream she hadn't realized she had. Someone whom she barely knew and yet somehow felt like she couldn't live without. Even if she would have to. Even, she thought, if she'd always planned to.

"And miss the sunset?" Lisa protested.

Ashley wavered, thinking that Lisa was right, that it would be a shame to go upstairs, shut the door to her room that faced the back of the house, not the front, and close her eyes to one of the best experiences the cottage offered.

She sat back down and picked up her wineglass. "You're right. And we won't have many more opportunities."

Lisa's brow pinched on that statement, and for a moment Ashley wondered if she was having second thoughts about selling the old place and if this was a safe opportunity for Ashley to voice her own concerns.

But before she could think of a way to broach that, Lisa smiled and looked out over the water. "All the more reason to make the most of each day. I've forgotten a lot about this place over the years, but these sunsets are unforgettable."

They were. But somehow, Ashley had even managed to forget them. Once, she would have considered that a success. Now, she felt like she'd abandoned something she should have treasured.

Rachel, however, hesitated. For a moment, Ashley wondered if she'd hit a nerve, but she shook that off. Rachel didn't do feelings, not in the way that Ashley did. She didn't cry, whereas Ashley was known to blubber. She rarely even laughed, come to think of it. Rachel was stoic. This was something that Ashley had always liked about her, but now she felt agitated.

She didn't know her sister's innermost thoughts, and this had nothing to do with her living in New York or rarely calling. Rachel wasn't just quiet and pensive. She was deeply private. Even with her own sisters.

She never showed any weakness. Until last night.

Or maybe, it wasn't weakness at all. Maybe, opening your heart and daring to let someone in, without any guarantees that they'd stand by you, was the bravest thing anyone could do.

"I think," Ashley began, and then stopped herself. "I think that we should do something about Mom's journal."

"You mean read it?" Lisa looked both intrigued and horrified.

"Not all of it. But just a few pages. Or would that be wrong?"

There was silence around the table as the women pondered this. It was Rachel who finally spoke.

"I think we should only read the last few pages. Maybe it will help us to understand what went on that last summer. Maybe it will help us to say goodbye to this place."

Lisa chewed on her bottom lip and then went into the house, returning only a moment later with the notebook clasped in both her hands. She took her seat and set the journal on the center of the table, leaving them to all stare at it.

Finally, because Ashley couldn't stand the tension, she grabbed the book and turned it over, pulling open the back cover and flipping to the final entry. It was dated August, sixteen years ago. Her pulse kicked up when she saw her mother's familiar handwriting, so much better than her own had ever been. She wrote only with blue ink, in careful strokes, leading Ashley to believe that she took time with each entry, that she didn't waste her thoughts or feed into emotions the way she seemed so prone to do in recent years.

"If I'm being honest with myself, I haven't been happy with Bill in so many years that I can't remember the last time I was happy," she began, then glanced up at her sisters, wondering if she should stop. Both of them stared at her with knitted brows, echoing the same confusion she felt. "Happiness to me has become my girls. Their laughter. Their joy. Their dreams. I worry about them, of course. Lisa has fallen in love, but I worry that she's giving her heart away too quickly and that she'll face obstacles that she isn't yet prepared to handle."

Ashley stopped again. Lisa just pinched her lips and gave a silent nod.

Ashley continued. "Rachel is already an adult, even though she's still a child. She's so smart and so pensive, that I hope one day she lets herself go, gives her heart away, trusts that someone will love her just as she is."

Ashley swallowed hard, bracing herself for what came next. "And Ashley, my funny, carefree girl. So strong and stubborn. She wears her heart for all to see, and oh, that's a dangerous thing, but I wouldn't wish it to be any other way."

Ashley felt her breath catch and blinked a few times before moving on to the last paragraph.

"There are few guarantees in life, but my girls have been one of them. And the other is this house. It is here that I am myself. It is here that I can watch my girls run and play and bond and be their true selves, without all that other stuff that life brings us thrown in to muddle it all up. I can only wish that my girls stay like this forever, even if it's only in their memories. And I can only wish for myself that someday I will again be as happy as I am right now, in this house, sitting on the porch, watching a magnificent sunset, and feeling like just for a moment, even if it's just a moment, I have everything I need."

Ashley closed the book and set it on the table and then wiped a tear away. Lisa did the same, and even Rachel looked a little blotchy.

"She really knew us," Rachel said. "The parts of us that we didn't even understand at the time."

"All this time I felt like she let us down, but now I feel like we let her down. Or at least I did." Ashley sniffed. "I don't put myself out there anymore. I don't live with abandon. I shut people out. I shut out the possibility of love. I... shut you two out."

"We're all to blame for that," Rachel said, giving her a kind smile before turning to Lisa. "I haven't been there for you. Haven't made the time. I'm sorry."

"You don't me an apology. I've been wrapped up with my new family. It's not easy to stay in touch or stay close. But that's no excuse, at least not for me." Lisa tipped her head at Ashley. "I stopped being there for you when you needed me the most. Can you ever forgive me?"

Now Ashley smiled, all the way from her heart. "I already have. But now I'm really left wondering... Can we forgive Mom?"

There was a long silence, one of those kinds that only ever existed in this house, where they gathered every summer to escape the noise and energy of the city, to find peace. And quiet.

Ashley didn't need to say anything more and neither did her sisters. They'd heard enough. They knew what they wanted. And what they needed.

* * *

Because Ashley had always been closest to her mother, it made sense for her to be the one to make the call. She went into town the next day with a sense of purpose, a skip in her step that she recognized as hope. Usually, she'd put that in check quickly, remind herself of all the times her mother had let her down, how you couldn't depend on anyone to respond to a situation the way you wanted or match your feelings for them. But she didn't want to live like that anymore.

She wanted to be the girl her mother described in her journal. The girl who lived with all her heart. The girl she used to be, not the one she was afraid to be.

"Ashley!"

She stopped walking, her stomach tightening because she recognized the voice. She was two blocks away from Main Street and just around the corner from the Cottage Coffeehouse where she planned to stop and get some guaranteed cell reception.

But it seemed that she wasn't the only one who had that idea.

"Hey, Mack," she said casually because there was no reason to not be civil. She'd known what she was getting into with him, what he was all about. He'd never promised otherwise, and his reputation was well known, even by him, it would seem.

"I've been hoping to run into you," he said, frowning as he approached. "The way you left the other night, I was worried that something had happened."

She pulled in a breath as he came to stand in front of her, his eyes soft and searching, his face still as handsome as ever, but then, lots of men had handsome faces.

But no other man—until now—had something else. Her heart.

It was just a shame that she'd chosen to give it to someone who didn't want it. But then, she thought, thinking of Michael and how she'd probably hurt him in a similar way, there were some things in life that no one could control.

And Mack hadn't hurt her on purpose.

"It's been a busy time, with my sisters, and the house. I'm actually heading into the coffee shop now to tie up the last few strings."

"Can I join you?"

She hesitated for a moment, because it would be so easy to say sure, why not. They could spend an afternoon together, laugh, talk, maybe even more than that... But living for the moment no longer held the same appeal, not when, for the first time in a long time, she dared to hope for a future.

"What would be the point?" she said frankly.

"Because you're leaving?"

"Because I don't think we're looking for the same thing." Ashley shifted the weight on her feet, even though she didn't feel restless. She didn't have the urge to hurry away as quickly as possible, but she didn't have the desire to stand here wishing for something that would never happen either. Honesty was always her policy—and it applied here, too. Only this time, the truth was more difficult to say. "We've had fun. But you saw me as a girl who walked into your bar, just like all the others. A girl who boarded the ferry and would board it again. And I...well, I guess I saw you as something more."

Something flicked through his gaze and Ashley was almost impressed that he hadn't taken off running by now. Three weeks ago, that's exactly what she'd wanted to do when Michael bore his feelings to her. That or toss herself into that chocolate fountain.

"I did think you were a girl who came over on the ferry and would board it again. All too soon," he said, catching her off guard.

She narrowed her eyes at him. "But I heard what you said. The other night. To that guy."

He squinted at her as if trying to recall. Really, did she need to spell it out for him?

"I won't deny any of what I said," he said simply. "But you only heard part of it."

Now it was her turn to narrow her eyes. "What do you mean, only part of it?"

"I'm guessing now from the way you left so suddenly that you only caught the part about me saying that the women I dated only lasted a short time. What you didn't hear me say was that now, I think that's a shame. Because I'd finally met a girl I didn't want to see go anywhere, not anytime soon. Not ever."

Ashley swallowed hard. "I guess I didn't hear you say that part."

Mack's mouth crooked into a grin. "Here I thought that was maybe the part that sent you running off, overpaying for a drink and everything."

"I did overpay for that drink," Ashley lamented. "But I wasn't going to stick around and break change. Or leave you hanging."

"You did leave me hanging," he said, lifting his eyebrows. "I thought maybe you'd left, back to New York. I thought maybe I'd never see you again."

"I'm right here," she said, giving him a slow grin. Her heart was beating so loudly that she was beginning to wonder if he could hear it, and she found that she didn't even mind. Let him know that she cared. Let him know that she dared to believe.

"I have a little time before I have to get to work," he said. "Do you want to get ice cream? A coffee? A walk?" He gave a bashful grin. "Really, I'd be fine with anything, so long as it includes you."

"I do," she said. "To all of those. And more."

But first, she had a call to make.

28

RACHEL

Rachel had a ritual when she was younger. Each year, on their last day of the summer, she went around to each room of the house before the furniture was draped or the clothes were completely packed, before the evidence that they had been there was covered up or stowed away for another winter. She took it all in, committing it to memory, and silently saying goodbye.

She kept the water for last. She'd cross the road, dodging the bicycles and people on horseback that occasionally ventured this far from town, usually only the locals, on their way to the other neighborhoods, up in the woods, or the cliffs. She'd dip her toes in, letting the water cover her feet, and then she'd select one stone, one that stood out amongst all the rest, and she'd make a wish before tossing it into the lake.

The last summer she'd been here, she'd written her wish down in her journal. Rachel had read through it all last night, tucked into her summer bed, alternating between laughing and—to her surprise—crying at the girl who was so very her, but a stranger all the same. A girl who had opinions on everyone, of course, who felt the need to remark on Ashley's endless splinters, to account for the details of the event, how Lisa would help their mother gather a bowl of warm water to soak Ashley's feet first, how her mother would sterilize the needle, how Rachel was sure her poor sister's screams could be heard all the way across the water to the mainland. And how afterward, there would be ice cream or pie, and they'd all sit outside on the porch and watch the fireflies dot the night sky, and how nothing, not even the drama of yet another splinter, could make any of them consider never returning again.

And that had been her wish that last year. A premonition perhaps, or just Rachel being Rachel, picking up on an undercurrent, on words that weren't yet spoken, on fear, perhaps.

She'd wished to someday return again to this house. As if it was no longer a given.

Today, though, her wish was for something else. Quietly, she walked through all the rooms, pausing to lift a framed photo, careful to set it back exactly where it was, knowing that it was her final day in this wonderful house. But it wasn't a house at all, really. It was home.

The sun was warm today and the sky was cloudless, creating that vision of the island she always had—one of bold blue clashing with vivid green. The road was quiet and she crossed it to the lakefront, taking her time to select the perfect stone, even if she knew it was just superstition. Something in her had to do it. Just like she had to follow through on her innermost desire. Her wish.

Her heart's truth.

Closing her eyes, she thought the words, carefully, deliberately, not wanting to mess anything up. She opened her eyes to toss the rock but a noise behind her made her turn. She wasn't alone this time.

"Marty?" She stared at her husband, not sure if he looked so out of place because he was here, on this island of all places, or because she hadn't dared to think of him enough.

Or because maybe, she hadn't looked at him enough. Not closely enough.

"What are you doing here?" she finally asked.

"Looking for you," he said, climbing over a boulder to step onto the gravel path. "I thought you were coming back last Sunday."

"I decided to stay longer. I didn't…I didn't think a few extra days would matter." It wasn't like they told each other every detail of their individual schedules. They lived parallel lives.

"It wouldn't," he said, looking affronted, "but didn't you think to tell me? I was worried."

She felt something in her flash. Something that went from being touched to being angry.

"I thought you'd be too busy to be worried."

"Well, of course, I'm busy. We both are." He narrowed his eyes at her. "Wait. What's this about?"

She tipped her head. It was bound to come up and it would have to be now. She took a steadying breath and tried to think of all the advice she gave her clients.

"I saw you. With a woman. The week before I came here. You said your flight wasn't getting in until nine, and I saw you, an hour before that, at a restaurant around the corner from our house."

He blinked, and at that moment, she knew the truth. She didn't need to hear another word, because she may not know how Marty spent his days, or what he ate for lunch Monday through Friday, but she knew his heart.

Marty hadn't cheated. Marty wouldn't think of cheating. And somewhere deep down inside of her, was a little girl who feared he would. And that there would be nothing she could do to stop it.

"I did get in early that night. But you had texted that you were having dinner with Lisa. I didn't want to go back to the apartment alone, so I stopped by the place on the corner. The new one. Thought I'd try out the menu before we went. Couldn't stand to listen to you complain if you didn't think their wine list was as good as Lawrence's." He gave a pained grin. "I ran into some old colleagues. Remember Jed and Stephanie?"

"Jed and Stephanie." Rachel felt her jaw slacken. Who could forget Jed and Stephanie? They'd always joked about them leaving to start their own tech business when really they were running off to get married. Steph, with her beautiful blond hair.

"Oh, Marty." She shook her head. "I'm sorry."

"No," he said firmly. "I'm sorry. You saw what you saw, anyone might have thought something. Especially when..."

"When what?" She was holding her breath, bracing

herself. This couldn't be the end. Not now, when she'd just found him again. Here on Evening Island of all places.

"Since you've been up here, I realized that we don't take any trips together."

"Well, we both have very busy schedules," she reminded him. "Important careers. People who are counting on us."

"But we're important. Or we should be. We are to me. We should be counting on each other. We should be prioritizing each other."

She pulled in a breath. "I couldn't agree more."

He sank his hands into the pockets of his khakis, which bore signs of wrinkles that were usually never there. "This is quite a place. I can't believe you never brought me up here."

"I can't believe I didn't either," she said softly, and then brushed away a tear. "But you're here now. I can share it with you now. If you'd like that."

His grin was broad, as warm and as kind and familiar as that old house across the road. It wasn't just a smile. It was home.

"I'd like that a lot," he said, reaching out to take her hand. "What's this?" he asked, tapping her hand that held the carefully selected stone.

"It's a wishing stone," she said, grinning.

"Don't let me stop you," he said, stepping back, but she dropped the rock to take his other hand instead.

"You don't need to," she whispered. "Because it already came true."

29
LISA

Lisa was doing one last walk through the back garden, stopping every so often to pluck a weed, even though she knew that it wouldn't make a difference at this point. They'd just find a way to grow back because most things in life were persistent like that. Her phone rang and her mind raced with the possibilities of what news it could bring—if the fate of this house had finally been decided—but the name that flashed on the screen only brought her calm. And joy.

"Maisie!" She'd been good about leaving her daughter alone these past few days, free to enjoy her experience to its fullest. Now, she refrained from asking if everything was okay, and instead reminded herself that she couldn't protect her child from everything in life—just like her own mother couldn't have.

"Are you still on the island?" Maisie asked.

Lisa sat down at the old wrought-iron café table near the rosebushes. "For now, but probably not much longer. The plans for the house are still..." She tried to find the right word and said, "Yet to be determined." Like everything else. "How's the trip going?"

"Fine. Fun. But I wish you were here. There's so much you'd love about it. So much I want to tell you about."

Lisa's smile was wan. "Oh, honey. I can't wait to hear about it. And we'll still go together. Just the two of us."

"That's what I told Dad, but I got the impression he felt left out."

Lisa fell silent. She'd thought she had done the right thing by still standing shoulder to shoulder with Steve over the years, and maybe she had, for Maisie. But not for herself.

"That's why I had him bring me out to the French restaurant before we came, just the two of us. So he felt like he could share in our passion, at least just a little."

Lisa frowned. "What French restaurant?"

"You know that fancy place, near the lake?"

Lisa's heart was thudding in her chest. "The bistro? When was that?"

"Right before I left for my trip. You should have heard him trying to speak French, Mom. I wish you'd been there."

I wish I had been too, Lisa thought. She stood, feeling the need to move, to walk toward something. Or maybe, someone.

"I'm glad you and your dad had that special time before you left. You'll be back soon enough and we'll have lots to share by then."

"I love you, Mom."

Lisa smiled. "I love you, too."

She hung up the phone and scrolled through her calls, her texts, the little notes from Steve that had built up over the years, their exchanges mostly about Maisie, of course, who always tied them together, but really, who kept them together.

But then her eyes fell on the last few since she'd been here. Steve wanting to know how she was. Steve checking in. Steve wanting to have dinner. Together. While Maisie was away.

Their relationship wasn't conventional. It wasn't even well defined, but what family wasn't a little messy, she thought, looking up at the big house and all the life it had witnessed over time.

* * *

"You don't mind driving back alone?" Rachel asked. "If you wait until tomorrow, Marty can take his car and I can ride with you."

"It's fine," Lisa assured her. "You and Marty deserve some time together, and it's time for me to get back home."

She carried her luggage down the winding steps, Rachel following close behind. "I have to say that I'm relieved we won't be selling this house."

It had been decided last night, on the porch, over wine and the promise that their mother would be returning, by herself. Of course, her latest relationship had recently ended, not that anyone was surprised. Only instead of falling apart as she had in the past, she'd shown a new emotion when Ashley posed the question. One that was now felt amongst them all.

Hope. The house had always held it, even if they hadn't experienced it for themselves. If their wounded hearts hadn't dared to believe that life could be better or go back to the way it was.

Maybe it couldn't, fully. But there were some things in the past that were worth fighting for, worth holding on to.

"What about your shop?" Rachel asked. "I know you were relying on the money from the sale of the house to keep it going."

Lisa had thought about this, of course, but it no longer kept her awake at night—and if it did, it was only because the change of plans excited her so much. "The shop is important to me, but this house is more important. Besides, being here gave me some new ideas for the place."

"Oh?" Ashley looked intrigued as she came in through the screen door.

"I was thinking about turning the shop into a consignment shop. Going through the attic and thinking about how each object told a story made me remember why I was also so intrigued by the history of this house. Each item in it felt special."

"Like a treasure," Ashley commented.

"Exactly," Lisa said. "I'm looking forward to it. To the future."

"And does that future include something else? Or rather, someone?" Rachel gave her sister a knowing look.

"I think it does," Lisa said, unable to hide her smile. She huffed out a breath and took a good look around the front hall, looking all the way up to the ceiling, where the signs of wear and neglect were completely repaired. Just like she was. "I'm sad to leave."

"You'll be back," Ashley promised. "And just think, next time you visit, Mom will be here too."

Lisa and Rachel exchanged a glance. The familiar sense of apprehension reared like it always did when their mother came up in more recent years. "Is it strange for me to hope that Mom will be her old self when we see her again?"

"If she's here, then I think you can do more than hope," Rachel said. "I think you can believe it."

"This house certainly has a way of bringing out the best in people." Lisa looked wistfully at Ellie's painting, still hanging over the mantle of the front room, where it belonged. "I can't wait to bring Maisie here for Gemma's wedding."

Ashley would be staying, here with their mother in the house, but Rachel and Marty would return for the event, and Lisa and Maisie, too. And maybe, hopefully, probably, Steve. They'd get to see Hope, Kim, Heather, and even Billy. She couldn't imagine missing it.

And she didn't want to miss more than she already had.

"It'll be the best reunion ever," Ashley said.

Lisa shook her head. "No," she said as she pulled her sisters in for a hug. "This has been the best reunion ever."

EPILOGUE

West End Road was full again—of laughter and music and joy and hope. This time, there weren't nine young girls, running free, their braids flying behind them, butterfly nets in their hands, but instead, larger, older, wiser versions of those girls, holding flower bouquets bound by satin ribbons.

When Gemma learned that her sisters, the Taylors, and the Andersons would all be returning to the island for her wedding, she'd seen no choice—and a perfect opportunity. One bride, and eight bridesmaids. It wasn't the small wedding that she'd planned—not that Ashley would have permitted such a thing in the first place—but it was the wedding she was meant to have.

The wedding that she could have only dreamed of.

Rose and Victoria, Hope Morgan's twins, were the flower girls, Ellie and Hope the joint maids of honor, and then there were the rest of them, the sisters in name only: Andrea, Heather, Kim, Lisa, Rachel, and Ashley. The summer sisters.

Some were missing, of course. Simon, Ellie's childhood crush and a regular around this part of the island, had gone a different path. And Mrs. Anderson, with her lovely, contagious, melodic laugh, was here in their thoughts and memories only, and sometimes, when the breeze caught the wind chime that still hung from the porch roof at the Anderson cottage, Lisa felt herself smile, thinking that maybe this was her way of saying she was still here. Somehow.

Because even when you left the island, a little piece of you remained, didn't it? Even when Lisa had tried to forget about the house, the water, and all these wonderful faces, they'd lived on, not just here, but in her heart, making it possible to reconnect as if no time had passed. As if another life, full of sadness and joy, heartache and hope, hadn't somehow interfered with those carefree moments spent and shared on this road.

There were new people now, of course. Hope's husband and her beautiful girls. John, who would likely propose to Andrea soon. Marty, of course, never knew how much he could love to ride a bicycle or enjoy sitting idle, doing nothing but sitting on the front porch, taking in the view of the water, and of course, Maisie. And Steve.

Lisa looked over at her husband now as she followed Kim Anderson down the aisle. Technically, Steve was still her ex-husband, but they were working on that. On making what they'd always known official. They were family. A complicated and unconventional one, but family all the same.

Leo Helms was standing at the wedding arch, the lake a beautiful dark blue behind him. It was one of those cloudless days that always came to mind when Lisa thought of the island, which was often these days, and not just because they'd all made the trek back here for the wedding.

Evening Island had welcomed her back, and it would again next summer, and the summer after that. There wouldn't be three-month visits, no, but there would be weeks here, sitting on the porch playing cards or eating pie from the bakery, biking into town, dipping her toes into the cold, clear water, taking in the comfort of the silence that couldn't be found anywhere else.

From his seat between Maisie and Mack, Steve grinned at her, and Lisa gave a little smile as she stood in her position, clutching her bouquet and watching as Ashley finished her walk. The island life suited her youngest sister. In the short time since she'd moved here, Ashley's skin was rosy and her eyes were bright. Taking part in every detail of this wedding hadn't hurt her online presence either, and she was running out of rebuffs for the commenters who asked when it was her turn.

Yesterday, when Mrs. Morgan had teasingly asked just that, Ashley could only blush and smile.

The string quartet from the big hotel had been hired for the wedding, and as they took a moment to pause and then began the wedding march, the crowd rose. All eyes turned to the row of homes on West End Road, where, on the porch of Sunset Cottage, a bride was taking her father's arm.

It was a new beginning for Gemma Morgan. A new beginning for them all.

Even, Lisa thought, as she caught her mother's eye in the crowd, and blinked back happy tears, for the ones she'd least expected.

ABOUT THE AUTHOR

Olivia Miles is a *USA Today* bestselling author of women's fiction and contemporary romance. She has frequently been ranked as an Amazon Top 100 author, and her books have appeared on several bestseller lists, including Amazon charts, Barnes and Noble, BookScan, and *USA Today*. Olivia lives on the shore of Lake Michigan with her family and an adorable pair of dogs.

Visit www.OliviaMilesBooks.com for more.

www.ingramcontent.com/pod-product-compliance
Lightning Source LLC
Chambersburg PA
CBHW010640300726
49022CB00041B/503

* 9 7 9 8 9 8 6 2 6 2 4 9 9 *